Dedication

For all those who follow their Muse
wherever it takes them.
And to Tom Thomson, may his soul rest
forever on his beloved painted lake.

The Tom Thomson Mystery
Canadian Historical Mysteries
~ Ontario

Nancy M Bell

Print ISBNs
Amazon print 9780228632429
BWL Print 9780228632436
Ingram Spark 9780228632443
Barnes & Noble 9780228632450

BWL Publishing Inc.

Books we love to write ...
Authors around the world.

http://bwlpublishing.ca

Copyright 2024 by Nancy M Bell
Edited by Victoria Chatham
Cover art by Michelle Lee

Author's Note

While this novel is based on historical facts, please keep in mind as you read that it is a work of fiction. Historical characters who were present at Canoe Lake and vicinity at the time of Tom Thomson's death are mentioned but their actions and words are purely of this author's imagination. Harriet Agnes St. George is a fictitious character of my creation, her interaction with others is fiction and not based on any historical facts. I hope this will alleviate confusion for anyone reading this who is familiar with the circumstances surrounding the mystery of Tom Thomson's death.

Table of Contents

Preface

Hello, let me introduce myself. I am Harriet Agnes St. George. I'm sure you're wondering what I have to do with Tom Thomson, or indeed, with the mystery surrounding his death. I'm a painter as well and the wilds of New Ontario, that which you now know of as Algonquin Park, is one of my favourite places to indulge my passion. Being the early 1900s is it unusual for a woman to wander about unchaperoned, and in the bush at that. But let me assure you, I am no ordinary woman. I like to think I'm the forerunner of a new breed of women who will strike out and demand to be allowed to reach their full potential without the mostly unwanted advice of some male figurehead. It is only in April of this year of our Lord, 1917, that women are allowed to vote. About time too, in my opinion.

Let's just say, it's a good thing my dear Great Aunt Lois left me a sizable amount of money in her will, in my name and solely in my control. Much to my father's anger and dismay. But I digress.

Tom Thomson and I used to haunt the same places and tramp the same paths and portages, sometimes alone and sometimes together. Winnie Trainor often accompanied one or both of us, most often Tom as she had a soft spot for the man. Winne wasn't a painter, but she did love to fish and was always happy to help portage. And she did have a yen for Tom, as I have mentioned.

So, leaving you with this bit of background information, I will endeavor to tell the tale of Tom Thomson's death and the aftermath as I know it. The subject is still a painful one for me, so as you will soon see, I have set the story down in third person rather than first. It's a way of distancing myself from the grief and the anger at the treachery that ended Tom's life and his career.

Chapter One

Harriet St. George stepped off the train at the Canoe Lake Station and smoothed down her skirts. Tipping her head back she took a deep breath of the sharp air of early May. It was so wonderful to be free from the restraints of her rather conservative family. Here at Canoe Lake, Harriet could dispense with the cumbersome skirts and traipse through the bush clad in trousers and a flannel shirt. Not to mention the much more comfortable boots she wore while in the woods exploring for the perfect site to set up her portable easel and paintbox. She loved the French name for her paintbox: *Pochade*. It rolled off the tongue so nicely. Harriet giggled and refrained from doing just that. The locals already thought she was a bit strange, well except for Winnie Trainor who also liked to gad about in trousers and spend hours fishing out on the lake.

Shaking her head, Harriet turned to collect her luggage, not much more than the aforementioned paintbox and a duffle stuffed with what she would need for a summer of painting and fishing in the Park. Hopefully, the Frasers of Mowat Lodge had received her telegram, and her room would be ready when she got there. With the paintbox in one hand and the duffle over her shoulder, she went in search of the park ranger, Mark Robinson, who kept track of all comings and goings in the Park and had promised to arrange her transport from the station to the Mowat Lodge.

The duffle was heavier than one would expect, but that weight made Harriet's heart light. Along with the few clothes stuffed haphazardly in the bottom, most of the room was taken up with her collection of oil paints, brushes, and thin wooden shingles that she intended to use painting *en plien aire*. She'd copied that trick from a fellow painter she'd met last summer. Tom Thomson tended to paint quickly, but with an accuracy and feel that Harriet envied, any place he found a scene in the woods that spoke to him he captured it on the shingle boards. Only later did he transform the rough painting on the board into a canvas. Usually over the winter when he returned to Toronto.

Someday, she promised herself. Someday women artists would be recognized as well as the men. She loved the vibrant new style that was developing in the Canadian art world. Slipping away from the traditional method of reproducing a scene in minute detail. The advent of photography was slowly making that form of art less popular. Thomson's use of colour and bold strokes of paint intrigued Harriet and she vowed to attempt to hone her own skills this summer.

"Oh, Mark. There you are," she greeted the tall, thin park ranger who stepped out of the station house.

"Miss St. George." Mark acknowledged her with a tiny bob of his head.

"Oh, please, it's Harriet," she chided him. "Once I ditch these skirts you'll be hard pressed to tell me from the locals." Harriet gazed at the thick bush and the pale blue early May sky, the lake where the ice was just beginning to break up. "I do love this place."

"Harriet, then, if you wish. I'm sure if your father was here he wouldn't approved of me being so familiar."

"Pish posh on my father. I'm free for the summer of his stuffy ideas of what is proper for a young lady." She giggled. "I have my Great Aunt Lois to thank for this freedom, she left me a generous inheritance with strict instructions to use it as my heart desired. And I desire to spend the summer here, in Algonquin Park, painting and fishing. Watching the stars and moon shining over the lake."

Mark rubbed a hand over the short whiskers on his face, unsure just how to respond to her comments. Instead, he took the pochade box from her hand and led the way off the platform. "I've arranged a ride for you with Shannon Fraser. He's here to collect the mail and is willing to take you back to Mowat Lodge with him for twenty-five cents."

"Twenty-five cents? Really? When I've already paid him for my room for the whole summer? You'd think the least he could do is provide me transportation to his lodge." Harrier sniffed. Shannon and Annie Fraser weren't her favourite people, but their lodge was right on the edge of Canoe Lake, which was most convenient, not to mention that Mowat Lodge was where Tom Thomson lived when he wasn't out in the bush painting or guiding fishing tours.

Robinson shrugged. "Surely you're not really surprised, Harriet. After spending all of August at their place last summer you must know what he's like."

"Sadly, that is true." Harriet followed Mark toward the converted hearse that Fraser used to transport customers and others from the lodge to the train station and back. "Anything for a penny," she muttered digging in her reticule for the required payment.

"Mister Fraser," she greeted the tall somewhat scruffy man who waited by the carriage.

"Miss St. George," he replied. "Mrs. Fraser has your room all ready for you. Let me take that." He reached for her duffle and paintbox.

"I can manage, thank you." She set the duffle on the floor of the carriage and stepped back to let Mark place the compact paintbox on the seat. Harriet gathered her skirts and stepped up into the high wheeled passenger compartment. "Thank you, Mark. I'm sure I'll be seeing you around."

"I'm sure you will." Mark pushed the door closed with a snick.

She waved out the open window when Shannon Fraser climbed onto the driver's bench and set the team in motion. Harriet kept one hand on her precious paintbox and gripped the window frame with the other. The road, if it could be called that, was rough and ill kept. The carriage jerked and bounced over and through the rutted half-frozen path. Early May in the north country was more than a bit behind the conditions in Old Ontario. She looked out the window at the sun-gilded trees just starting to show a sheen of green as their newly minted leaves began to emerge. A cluster of pussy willow bushes brushed against the side of the carriage, the grey buds softly glowing with a rosy blush.

Oh, how she longed to pull out the paints and capture that glorious montage of colour. Time enough for that, she told herself as the converted hearse jolted along. She should have asked Mark if Winnie Trainor had arrived yet. Sometimes Winnie came up in March, but it was usually a bit later. Her family owned a cabin on the lake, beside the two-story whitewashed cottage of the German-Americans who came up each summer. Harriet thought of Winnie as a comrade in arms, flouting the mores of stuffy

15

civilized society. Harriet's lip curled a little at the thought of civilized society. Winnie liked nothing better than to spend the day fishing or tramping through the bush. Although Harriet suspected the tramping through the bush might be motivated more by the chance that Winnie might come across Tom Thomson than any real interest in the surroundings.

Harriet gave a little sigh. Maybe she was being a bit harsh. Thomson certainly seemed to like the woman and was kind toward her anytime Harriet had seen them together the previous summer. For herself, Harriet liked the man. He was always willing to talk about painting with her and offering suggestions to improve her own work. She found his paintings fascinating and often studied the ones he left lying out to let the paint cure. Once last summer she'd come across him while out painting herself and they'd spent a glorious late August afternoon painting in silent accord. Harriet was very proud of the work she'd done that day, capturing not only the rough details dominated by the sun on the lake and the shades and shadows of the trees, but the essence of the scene. Even in the depths of winter when she'd pulled that particular painting out she'd felt the sun on her back and smelt the earthy, piney fragrance of the bush.

The carriage jolted to a halt breaking her out of her thoughts. When Fraser opened the carriage door she ignored his offer of help and jumped down on her own, turning to gather up her belongings.

"Annie's in the office. You can collect yer key from her." Fraser dismissed her with his usual brusque manner, leading the team toward the back of the lodge.

"Thank you," Harriet called after him, more for politeness' sake than because he actually deserved the sentiment. Picking up her belongings she made her way up to the entrance to Mowat Lodge and went in search of Annie Fraser, hoping she really was in the office and that Harriet wouldn't have to go looking for her.

Chapter Two

Harriet set her paintbox on the washstand in the narrow room before tossing the duffle onto the skinny bed. She made a note she'd have to see if Mark Robinson knew anyone with a spare wool blanket she could buy or borrow. The Frasers were notoriously skimpy on providing home comforts for their guests. Oh, for a price they could produce just about anything, but a person had to be prepared to pay that price and be skinned alive. Something Harriet wasn't willing to do. She gave a secret smile, there were ways and there were ways to get around the Frasers wanting to control every little thing, especially if those little things could be turned into a source of income for them.

She went to the narrow window and forced the window up an inch in its swollen frame. The sweet spring air was welcome to chase the musty scent from the room. Harriet shook her head while unpacking her few items of clothing. *You would think that airing out the room was the least Annie could have done.* Flicking back the threadbare quilt covering the bed, she shook the sheets and flipped the thin pillow hoping to dislodge any spiders or other insects that might have taken up residence, not to mention mice or other vermin. From past experience she knew Annie was an indifferent housekeeper at best. Satisfied that nothing was lurking, she remade the bed and shoved the duffle under the frame. Her fashionable heels clicked on the floorboards which creaked as she moved to the door and locked it. With swift movements Harriet shed the cumbersome skirts, petticoats and tight shirtwaist. Crumpling them into a ball she shoved them onto the narrow shelf running along the top of the ancient armoire. Time enough to worry about them once the end of August came around, or maybe, she considered, the end of September or October. The autumn colours of the bush must be spectacular. She clasped her hands in front of her waist for a moment, fingers itching to grasp a brush and capture the demise of the yet unfurled green spring leaves.

Laughing at her whimsy, Harriet stepped into a battered pair of trousers and pulled on a flannel shirt over a sweater. Sitting on the bed she stuck her feet into thick woolen socks and laced her comfortable boots. Making sure she'd left nothing personal lying about for Annie or Shannon's prying eyes, she unlocked the door and stepped into the hall. It took only a moment to lock the door and scan the hallway. It didn't look like many, if any, of the rooms were occupied yet, but it was still early in the season.

"I wonder if Tom has arrived yet," she mused out loud while her feet carried her toward the stairs at the end of the long hall. The siren call of the bush was upon her, and Harriet was eager to answer. There was still the matter of arranging for the rental of a canoe for the season and she looked forward to a spirited bout of bargaining with Shannon. Honestly, the man would charge for the air his guests breathed if he could figure out a way to do it. Grinning, Harriet jumped over the last two steps landing lightly and heading for the door.

"Hello, Annie," she called passing the tiny room that served as an office.

"Got everything you need?" The heavy set woman lifted her head from the papers on her desk. "For a few pennies extra I got soap and you can get more towels if you need 'em."

"I'm fine, Annie. But thank you." Harriet carried on her way, eager to be out of the gloomy interior and out in the brisk air, warmed somewhat by the afternoon sunlight.

She followed the path down to the docks. The ice was still covering most of the lake, but patches of open water were showing around the edges. A light wind brought the aroma of wet earth and the cold watery scent of the thawing ice. Harriet made her way down to the water's edge, boots sinking in the soft mud. She took a stick and poked at the thin layer of ice, fascinated as it broke apart into tiny crystal bits. The wind picked up, blowing hard enough to shift the decaying ice cover. To Harriet's delight soft tinkling music rose from the shattering crystals. She stood entranced until the wind changed direction and the ice settled into silence once more.

"If only I could capture this in my art, somehow evoke the sound of that ice and the cleansing breath of the wind. If only..." She backed out of the mud and climbed up on the dock to gaze across the lake toward the two islands visible in the near distance. Big Wapomeo and Little Wapomeo Islands. The name came from the Ojibway term for birds of sun and laughter. Harriet had asked one of the women from the nearby native community she'd come across one day last summer while crossing from Joe Lake portage back to Canoe Lake. "Birds of sun and laughter, how beautiful and lovely. Like the loons." She smiled. The haunting cry of the loons somehow spoke to the artist and poet in Harriet's heart. It was a sentiment she shared with Tom Thomson, they'd had a long conversation about the loons and the other avian species that abounded in the area last summer. It was the same day she'd first me Tom while wandering about in the bush looking for inspiration. Sighing, she turned away from the lake and headed back toward Mowat Lodge. She'd ask Annie, or Shannon if she couldn't avoid it, if either of them knew when Tom was planning to arrive. Winnie Trainor should show up soon afterward, of course.

Harriet liked the woman and they'd spent many hours tramping through the woods or sitting on the still lake in separate canoes watching the sunset paint the waters pink and salmon and saffron, fishing poles in hand and lines in the water.

Chapter Three

"Annie, hello." Harriet paused in the door of the office. The woman ensconced behind the overflowing desk grunted and didn't lift her head.

Clearing her throat, Harriet tried again. "I was wondering if the Trainors were in residence at their cottage yet?"

"Haven't seen hide nor hair of 'em," Annie replied without looking up.

"Are you expecting any of them to arrive in the near future?" she persisted in spite of the other woman's taciturn nature.

"Nope." Annie set down her pen and leveled her gaze at Harriet. "I don't imagine the daughter will be far behind once Tom shows up, though."

"Oh, thank you." Harriet backed out of the doorway and then paused. "Are you expecting Mr. Thomson soon then?"

Annie's eyes narrowed and her fact took on a calculating expression. "That's the way the wind blows, is it?"

Harriet's face heated, but she firmed her jaw. "Not at all, I assure you. I'm merely inquiring as I'd like to take some lessons from him this summer. I do value his advice and I'm intrigued by the direction his art is going."

"Yeah, yeah, yeah." Annie waved her away with a meaty hand. "You just keep telling yourself that. And if I were you I wouldn't let Winnie know you're interested in Tom."

"I assure you my interest is only in his work, nothing else." Harriet pivoted on her heel and marched down the hall toward the staircase.

"Honestly, the nerve of that woman," Harriet fumed as she stamped up the stairs in a far from ladylike manner. At the top of the steps, she turned and regarded the mud tracks left by her boots on the risers. No doubt she'd hear about that from Annie as well, but the fact the other woman would have to clean up the mess brought a grim smile to Harriet's face. Reaching her room, Harriet unlocked the door and crossed the room to push aside the curtain at the window. The May sun was high in the sky now, visible above the thick growth of trees on the east side of the lake.

"Perfect." She nodded at her faint reflection in the smudged glass. It took only moments to gather up her painting box and small tin of insect repellant. She wrinkled her nose at smell of the bear grease mixed with sweetgrass and pineapple weed, which Harriet recognized as wild chamomile. Twisting open the tin, she smeared some ointment on every bit of exposed flesh she could find. She might stink to the high heavens but hopefully the pungent ordour would keep the swarms of blackflies away. The tiny insects would find the smallest opening in any protective clothing and feast to their little hearts' content. Thankfully they only lasted until the temperatures rose in early June.

Suitably armoured, Harriet hurried down the stairs and out the door. Taking a path she'd used many times the past summer she struck off into the bush. She knew just the place to catch the play of sun and shadow on the lake and itched to try and capture not only the image but the essence of the place as well. Recapture that feeling of breathing life into her painting she'd experienced last summer.

A half hour later she reached her destination and after swiping ineffectually at the annoying insects, Harriet set her paintbox on a convenient fallen log and perched on a curving cedar root. Small 8 by 12 shingle board propped in lid of the open pochade, Harriet set about mixing her paints on the handheld palette before sketching in the outline of the scene she intended to capture. Swift broad strokes of colour followed, nothing like the intricate, almost photographic, images the traditional artists were producing. While that technique was the accepted method, Harriet loved the way Tom's creations seemed to breathe with the life of his subjects and had adopted his unique style. She kept at her painting until the light began to fade. Setting down her brushes, Harriet stood and stretched her stiff back and legs. She moved back a few steps to regard the results of her labour. Not half bad, if she did have to say so herself. The sun was dipping behind the trees, the maples and hemlocks throwing long shadows across the lake. She rubbed her tired fingers together in an attempt to mitigate the increasing chill of the air. It might be May and warm down in Toronto, but here in the bush around Mowat in New Ontario winter's breath still held sway.

"Time to pack up and see what I can find for supper," Harriet said to the darkening woods where shadows gathered around the bushes. She made short work of cleaning her brushes and stowing the palette in the paintbox. The still wet painting she set into the clamps in the top of the box where it wouldn't get smeared. Once she got back to Mowat Lodge she would set it out to cure while she ate.

The trek through the bush took longer than she anticipated. The long day was catching up with her, but she was thrilled with her efforts to capture the essence of the light on the trees and lake. Emerging from the head of the trail she hiked across the Gilmour Lumber chip yard and was soon mounting the steps of the lodge. Hitching the paintbox up with one hand Harriet took the stairs two at a time. Once in her room she removed the board and set it on the windowsill. Stepping away from it for a better perspective she was pleased with the effect her broad brushstrokes had produced. She could hardly wait to show Tom and get his opinion and advice.

Taking a moment to tidy her hair which seemed to have collected its fair share of leaves and twigs, she smoothed the blonde strands away from her face and jammed a battered brimmed hat on her head. Viewing the image in the mirror Harriet allowed herself a chuckle. Father would have kittens if he ever saw her like this, but Great Aunt Lois would heartily approve. Whistling, she left the room, careful to lock the door behind her, and went in search of food.

* * *

The dining room, if the room sparsely furnished area could be called that, two men sat hunched over a table. There was something furtive about their movements, Harriet recognized Shannon Fraser as one of the men, the other was a stranger. How odd, she thought. I wonder what Shan is up to now. The man always seemed to have some scheme or another on the fire. She shrugged mentally, none of her business, thank goodness.

Harriet picked up a tin plate from the pile on the long table by the side of the room and regarded the offerings. Pickles and cheese, biscuits and butter, some meat that she thought was venison. Piling some of each on the plate Harriet took it to a table by the wide windows and then sauntered over to pour herself a cup of coffee with the consistency of mud. A generous helping of sugar made the liquid more palatable. Crossing behind the two men, she caught a wisp of the conversation which made her steps falter. Before they could realize she'd overhead anything, Harriet hastened back to her table.

Interesting, they mentioned Tom and then something I didn't catch. But I'm sure I heard Shan asking when the next shipment was coming. I hope Tom isn't caught up in any of Shan's schemes. Shipment of what? I'd bet my bottom dollar it's bootleg whisky, there certainly seems to be no shortage of that around here. I wonder if Mark Robinson, the park ranger, is aware. I can't imagine he's in on anything.

In spite of the direction of her thoughts, Harriet finished eating quickly. Setting the plate where Annie insisted they go in the bin by the kitchen, she poured another cup of coffee and took herself outside to watch the sunset. Throwing her head back, Harriet let the blended colours of the sky wash over her, the golds and reds and salmons faded to mauve and saffron, then blended with the newly minted green of the bush as the sun hid its face behind the tree line. This early in the year, darkness came early and the air chilled quickly. The lonely cry of the train coming into Canoe Station echoed through the stillness as she drained the last of the coffee from the cup. She wandered back into the lodge and decided to bring her book down and read in the lobby for a while, just in case Winnie or Tom was a passenger on the newly arrived train. It wouldn't take too much time for them to make their way from Canoe Lake Station to Mowat Lodge.

Twenty minutes later boots echoed on the wooden steps and the lodge door swung open. The man stopped in the doorway to let his eyes adjust to the lamp light. He dumped a satchel on the floor by his feet, took his hat off and swept the hair from his forehead. Jamming the hat back over his unruly hair, the man stooped to retrieve his bag. In doing so, his gaze landed on Harriet.

"Hetty, is that you?" Tom Thomson straightened up and crossed the floor toward her after removing his hat and jamming it under his arm.

"Hello, Tom. Yes, it's me. I just got here today, but I managed to get a bit of time in the bush with my paints already. I can't wait to get your feedback on it." She stood, dropping the book into the chair behind her. A tiny flame of warmth flickered in her chest, nobody called her Hetty except Tom.

"It's great to see you. I have to admit I didn't expect to see you this early in the season." He extended his right hand and clasped hers.

She returned the grip and released his hand. "I couldn't wait another minute. Father was driving me crazy, hinting and then insisting it was way past time I was married and taken off his hands." She grinned. "So, I took myself off his hands."

Tom grinned in return. "I can see that." He cocked his head to the side and regarded her, eyes shadowed by the flop of hair across his forehead. "Somehow I can't picture you married and fussing around a house all day."

"No more than I can," Harriet agreed. "Hence my presence here before the ice has left the lake." She paused. "Although I suppose I'll have to marry someday…maybe. But let's not waste time talking about that right now. What have you been up to all winter?"

"Oh, this and that. Do you remember the sketch of the pine tree, the twisted one on the rock?"

"Of course, I loved that one. So much strength and beauty in it." Harriet clapped her hands.

"I finished the larger canvas of that this winter and worked on a few other things. I've had a bit of luck selling some of my work as well, so I'm not as skint this summer as last." He stretched his arms over his head. "It's so good to back here where a man can breathe and the sky isn't blocked by buildings."

"Amen to that," Harriet agreed. "Did Shan know you were coming today? If not you'll have to find Annie and get a room sorted."

"I sent a telegram, but you know how things go here sometimes." Tom shrugged. He turned back and shouldered his duffle bag. "I suppose I'll go beard the dragon in her den." He grinned and moved toward the office. "Good night, Hetty."

"Good night, Tom." She picked up her book and moved toward the stairs. "Tom," she paused at the foot, "have you heard from Winnie? Do you know when she's planning on arriving?"

The tall man turned back to her, looking down from his height of six-feet. "I have no idea, I haven't heard from Winne all winter. But then I've been busy and moving around a bit, I could have missed a letter I suppose. I'm sure she'll turn up before too long." He continued toward the closed office door.

"I suppose," Harriet echoed before going in search of Shan in order to settle the matter of the canoe rental for the summer. The negotiations took far longer than she expected, but in the end she was happy with the deal she'd struck. *Never underestimate the power of a determined woman. Not to mention a stubborn one.* Harriet giggled as she mounted the stairs and entered her room. The faint moonlight threw the rough ridges of her oils into sharp relief when she looked at her afternoon's work. The play of light and shadow gave a new dimension to the painting, and she spent a few minutes studying it from different perspective points while moving around the room. "I think it's good. I mean really good," she whispered hugging her arms around her waist. "I hope Tom will think so. He might be inclined to mention me to some of his supporters. Wouldn't that be a triumph, if I could actually get recognition for my painting and maybe even sell some." She giggled. "Father would really have kittens then."

Harriet lit the lamp on the dresser and undressed quickly in the unheated room. She pulled on the flannel pyjamas she favoured rather than the voluminous night rail her mother and sisters slept in. Blowing out the lamp she slid into the bed, wrapping the blanket around her and shivering until her body warmth heated the bed enough she could sleep.

Chapter Four

The last days of May passed far too quickly for Harriet. She spent most of her time in the bush or paddling the canoe she'd decided to rent from the Algonquin Lodge rather than the Frasers after discovering it was less than half the price Shan would have charged. That hadn't endeared her to the Frasers, but she didn't care too much about that. Even though she wanted to spend every minute she could with a brush in her hand, the need to soak in the solace and solitude of the wilderness was stronger. The weather was warming as May slid into June, the blackflies were replaced by swarms of mosquitoes and deer flies. The insects often drove Harriet out of the shade of the trees and onto the lake where the strengthening sun kept the flies at bay a bit.

* * *

The breeze tugged at the ribbon binding her long hair back at the nape of her neck, Harriet raised her face and closed her eyes, basking in the sun which stood high overhead. Her canoe floated near the shore where the Trainor's cottage was located. Leaning her paddle across the gunwales Harriet glanced toward the building in an attempt to ascertain if any of the Trainors had arrived. It was unlikely given the fact anyone arriving by train would have been known to the residents of Mowat. She was sure Annie would have had something to say about Winnie showing up. Still, Harriet wasn't spending much time at the lodge, rising early and staying either in the bush or on the water until the light faded. Taking up the paddle she moved the canoe out further into the lake, enjoying the pull of the water against the flexing of her muscles as the narrow vessel slid through the water. There was an east wind blowing and small whitecaps slapped at the canvas sides but caused her no trouble. After a few lessons from Tom last summer Harriet considered herself a proficient paddler.

She made her way toward Little Wapomeo Island, the breeze cooling the sweat gathering on her face and between her shoulder blades. The sun picked diamonds from the small chop of the water, and she shipped her paddle again. In the lee of the island, she let the canoe float and fished behind her seat for a shingle. In order to paint while on the lakes, Harriet had rigged a makeshift place for her paintbox. She opened the lid and set the blank board in place, preparing to try and capture the play of light and colour, the sky reflecting on the water with fragments of clouds wisping across the blue. She blocked in the bulk of island trees and the straggle of rocks on the point, leaving the majority of the space for the sky and water with the far shoreline a counterpoint in the distance.

"Hetty!"

The sudden call startled her so she almost dropped her brush into the lake. Gripping the gunwale to steady the canoe, she turned her head toward the sound. The peculiar grey-green colour of the canoe rounding the point identified the paddler as Tom.

"Hey," she called back. "You startled me. I thought you were up at Tea Lake Dam." She waited while Tom paddled the short distance, sculling with his paddle to bring his canoe alongside hers with only a slight bump.

"What are you up to? I figured you'd be out in the bush or painting somewhere, not lazing about in the sun," Tom teased, sunlight glinting off his rugged features.

"I am painting," she insisted, pointing at the crate fixed to the bottom of the canoe which held her paintbox.

"That's ingenious, I wish I'd thought of it." Tom leaned over to study what she'd done. "I might have to figure something out for my canoe. I see you've been working on your style." He nodded at the two completed paintings she'd set on the bow seat of the canoe to cure in the sun.

Warmed by his praise, she smiled and placed a hand over his where it held the gunwale of her canoe to keep them from drifting apart. "Thank you. I thought if I could paint on the water it might give a different perspective to my work. And it's so peaceful just floating on the lake, like I'm actually part of the painting, in it I mean, not just putting down what I see." Harriet gave a self-depreciating laugh and removed her hand. "That sounds really pretentious, doesn't it?"

"Not at all, Hetty." Tom's face was serious. "I know exactly what you mean, about being part of the painting, not just the creator of it. If it's all right with you, I think I'm going to see if I can rig something up like your idea so I can try painting from the canoe."

"Of course, you're welcome to it. The only thing I can tell you from my experience is that the wind can be tricky, and if the water is even a bit rougher than it is now the whole thing is an effort in futility. I almost got blown into Big Wapomeo the other day because I wasn't paying attention and then the wind caught me broadside," she shrugged, "and you know how that goes."

"Well, just be sure to be careful, Hetty. I don't want to find your canoe floating upside down and you in the drink."

"I learned my lesson, I assure you," Harriet said. "Hey, do you know when Winnie is coming? I thought she'd be here by now. Did you stop in Huntsville on your way up here? I forgot to ask you before."

Tom looked down at his hand holding the paddle across the canoe. "She's coming up on the afternoon train. That's the last I heard. Today is June sixth, isn't it?" He raised his gaze to her face.

"Yes, I believe it is. Oh, I'm glad. I can't wait to see her. It will be nice to have some female company, well besides Annie Fraser." Harriet grinned.

"I see your point," Tom agreed.

"Are you going to meet her at the train or at the Lodge. I suppose they must have their boat stored there."

"I hadn't planned on it. I'm sure she'll have settling in to do, and her father will be with her to help with things. I'm headed over to Joe Lake to see if I have any luck catching that big trout we've all been after. Wish me luck!" Tom let go of the gunwale and backed his canoe away from Harriet's. With a brief wave, he paddled off toward the portage over to Joe Lake.

"Well, that's interesting. I wonder what Annie will make of Tom not being around when Winnie arrives. I'm sure that woman is reading my mail from some the things she's inadvertently let drop while she's busy gossiping. Like how did she know my father forbade my youngest sister to come up for a visit? I surely never mentioned it, but Amelia did write to me to complain about Father. I bet she reads everyone's mail, including Tom."

During the brief exchange with Tom, the light had changed. With quick strokes Harriet filled in the scene as best she could, vowing to work on it a bit more later tonight in her room. It might not be as vibrant as if she could have completed it here on the water, but the sketch had enough body to warrant continuing to work on it. Slipping the panel into the clamps on the box, she stowed the other two panels as well and closed the box. Dipping the paddle into the water she turned the canoe and went in the opposite direction from the Joe Lake portage. One woman chasing after Tom Thomson was enough, Harriet had no intention of adding her name to the list.

It was only mid-afternoon, but Harriet changed direction and turned the bow of her canoe toward the dock at Mowat. The wind was coming up and there might be time to make a short excursion into the bush. There was a certain grove of birch trees that stood in sharp relief against the backdrop of dark spruce and tamarack that she had her eye on. After that, she'd wait around to meet Winnie when the train came in. Harriet pulled her canoe up above the waterline and turned it over to let the canvas over the cedar strip dry. Shouldering her paddle, she carried it up to her room. There was no point in taking the chance of the paddle walking off on its own if she left it with the canoe. It happened twice last summer and there was no way Harriet was going to allow that to happen again. She was pretty sure she'd bought her own paddle back twice from the Frasers.

Stowing it under her bed, she locked the door and skipped down the stairs, pausing as she passed the dining room. Shannon Fraser was bent over a table engrossed in an intense conversation with another man. The second man had his hat pulled down over his face, Harriet was fairly sure she had seen him hanging around after dusk on more than one occasion. She tucked herself up against the wall and peered around the door frame into time to see Fraser hand over a wad of bills which the other man tucked in his jacket pocket. The two men stood up and Harriet scurried away from her vantage point. She was still close enough to hear their conversation as they left the dining room.

"You'll be sure to make the delivery tonight," Fraser growled.

The second man muttered something and nodded his head.

"You know the meeting place, they'll be waiting by the time you get there. Don't be late, and don't screw anyone over. I find out you're sampling the product there'll be hell to pay." Shannon cuffed the shorter man on the shoulder.

Harriet cleared her throat and made it look like she'd just come down the stairs, her boot heels sounding loud on the floorboards. Whatever clandestine activities were going on, she didn't want to get caught up in it. If she had to guess, they were probably selling bootleg liquor to the natives. There was no doubt there was no shortage of booze at the lodge. Most nights saw the men gathered around the big firepit outside passing the jug. Sometimes Annie joined them. Maybe, Harriet thought, I should go the next time Annie decides to join, or even better, I bet Winnie will be up for it. Especially if Tom is there. "Not that it's any of my business," she reminded herself while slipping out the door and heading for her favourite trail in search of that elusive grove of birch trees.

* * *

The sky had darkened to an ebony blue with the first starts pricking the firmament when Harriet made her way back to Mowat Lodge.

"Damn, I've probably missed Winnie by now." She kicked a stone out of the path where it landed with a satisfying plunk in the shallow water of the lake. A smile slid across her face though. Safely tucked in the paintbox in her hand was the rough sketch of the birch grove. It was good enough, in her opinion, to turn it into a larger piece on canvas. Her step slowed, but first, before she got too excited, she would show it to Tom and see what he thought of her work.

The lamp light from the lodge hall sent warm yellow light into the gloom. Harriet blinked to let her eyes adjust to the change in light.

"Harriet! There you are!"

A body almost bowled Harriet over and she clutched the precious paintbox tightly. Strong arms enfolded her, lifting her almost off her feet.

"Winnie! I wanted to be here to meet you, but I got involved with this painting I was working on, and the time just slipped away from me." Harriet caught her breath as Winnie released her.

"Figures," Winnie sniffed, "you and Tom, both of you. I think you like your paintings more than you like me."

"Oh Winnie. You know that's not true. I love spending time with you, and I'm sure Tom does too."

"Where is he?" Winnie squinted over Harriet's shoulder. "When he wasn't here I thought he must be with you somewhere."

Harriet shook her head and taking Winnie's arm drew her into the lodge and out of the worst of the mosquitoes that were swarming to the lamp light. "I spoke with him earlier out on the lake. He was headed to Joe Lake to try for that big trout the men are all het up about."

"Do you expect him back tonight?" Winnie settled on a chair in the hall by the dark dining room.

"I hardly know. I don't keep track of his whereabouts. If I had to guess, I'd say he's probably going to camp somewhere and try for the fish early in the morning if he doesn't have any luck today. You know him and Mark Robinson and mostly likely Shannon have a bet going on over who is going to land that thing."

"I was hoping he'd be here to greet me. I sent him a telegram letting him know I'd be on the afternoon train." Winnie's lower lip pouted and a frown creased her forehead. She shot a glance at the closed office door. "I bet Annie never even gave it to him." Winnie pushed herself up from the cushioned chair.

Harriet put a hand on her arm and pulled her back down. "He must have gotten the telegram because he told me you were expected on the afternoon trail. There's no point antagonizing Annie when Tom must have read it."

"Hummf." Winnie blew her breath out in a huff. "That man. Sometimes I don't know why I bother."

"I'm sure he'll show up sometime tomorrow," Harriet soother her friend. "Are you staying here tonight? I would have thought you'd go across to the cottage."

"Father isn't coming until tomorrow and I decided to wait for him. There's a fair bit of work to do opening up the cottage for the summer. I only came up a day early because I was hoping to spend some time with Tom."

"I'm sorry." Harriet patted her arm. "Have you had a bite to eat?"

Winnie nodded. "I managed to get something from Annie when I arrived. You'd think I'd asked for the moon, the look she gave me."

"I can imagine." Harriet grinned. "I have a stash of food in my room just I never have to rely on the Frasers. In a tin box," she added, "no point in feeding the rodents."

"Smart lady," Winnie said getting to her feet. "Since there's no chance of seeing Tom tonight, I think I will turn in. Travelling on the train always tires me out. See you in the morning at breakfast?"

"Of course." Harriet linked her arm with Winnie's. "I'm ready to turn in too. It's been a long day, and I need to set my latest painting out to cure." She patted the paintbox.

The two women went up the wide staircase arm in arm, Harriet keeping the paintbox safely in her free hand. They parted ways at Harriet's door, Winnie disappeared into the room two doors down.

Chapter Five

Harriet sat on the steps of the lodge nursing a cup of coffee and listening to Winnie complain that Tom hadn't returned yet.

"He knew I was coming and it's been almost a week," Winnie grumbled, sighing and leaning back to tip her face to the sun.

"You know what he's like when he's painting or tramping through the bush. He forgets what year it is let alone what day," Harriet soothed her. Personally, she thought if Winnie was dogging her footsteps as much as she did Tom's Harriet would be sorely tempted to disappear into the bush too. "Have you got the cottage all set up for the summer," she sought to change the subject.

"Pretty much," Winnie nodded, "Father arrived five days ago and has done most of the heavy stuff, I've got the beds all aired and swept out the dust." She paused and grimaced. "The Blechers are supposed to arrive today or tomorrow. I hope Tom and Martin Jr. don't get into it over the war."

"They're the German-Americans with the cottage not far from yours?" Harriet tried to put faces to the name."

"That's right."

"I didn't realize Tom and Martin don't get along. Surely nothing serious, I hope."

Winnie shrugged. "Martin Jr is just so opinionated, and he tends to side with the Germans when the men start talking about the war. You can imagine how well that goes over."

"Is Martin Sr. as opinionated? Or his sister? What was her name?" Harriet wrinkled her brow.

"Bessie. She's a quiet sort, always hanging around with Martin Jr. I've tried to be friendly to her, but she doesn't seem interested. Very much keeps to herself and her immediate family that one. And don't even ask me about the mother. She can be mean as a cornered badger, that on."

"Hmmm," Harriet murmured for want of something better to say. A flash of sunlight on a paddle drew her gaze to the far side of Canoe Lake. She squinted against the sun bouncing off the water and stood up. "Looks like Tom's canoe." She pointed toward the peculiar coloured canoe approaching toward the Mowat dock.

"Well, it's about time." Winnie got to her feet and started toward the dock with a determined stride.

Harriet subsided back unto the step and sipped the remains of her coffee. She was anxious to show Tom her sketch of the birch grove, but no way did she intend to get herself in the middle of what looked to be a lover's quarrel. Tipping the last of her coffee unto the ground, she got up and sauntered into the main hall of the lodge.

"Looks like Tom Thomson is back from his latest excursion," she commented to Annie as she passed the open office door.

"Hummpf," Annie snorted, "I suppose that Trainor girl has hightailed down to meet him." She shook her head. "Wasting her time, that one."

"What do you mean?" Harriet leaned on the door frame dangling the empty coffee cup from her index finger. "He seems to like her well enough."

"That may be, but that man's ain't the marryin' type and marryin' is what Winnie Trainor has in mind."

"I thought they had an 'understanding'?" Harriet indulged her curiosity with a little gossip.

"If an 'understanding' means she's at his beck and call when he has a mind for it, I guess you're right. But he ain't lookin' for anything permanent." Annie sniffed. "And if he was, he could do better than her." She turned back to whatever was on her desk, effectively ending the conversation.

Harriet continued to the dining room to leave her cup and then mounted the stairs to her room to collect her paintbox. She left the birch grove study still curing on the windowsill, locked the door and headed for the stairs. The sound of voices stopped her at the top. Whatever Shannon and Annie were discussing seemed to be pretty serious and from the tone of their voices something they didn't want anyone else to overhear. Carefully stepping down unto the first riser, she peered through the railing while keeping herself in the shadows.

"Tom's back. You'll need to talk to him about—"

"I know what I need to do. Hush your trap woman. Anybody could be listening."

"The only one in the lodge right now is that St. George woman and she's up in her room. I just saw her go us a moment ago."

"Still. You gotta be careful. We got a good thing goin' with the Indians and using that trapper guy keeps our hands clean. Nothin' to connect us with anything. Certainly not bootleg whiskey." Shannon's features took on an innocent air. "No need to get the supplier concerned either. We don't' want to cross that crowd."

"Just be sure you talk with Thomson. Make sure he don't know nothin'. And if he does, make sure he ain't gonna do anything about it." Annie glared at her husband and disappeared into her office.

Harriet slunk back up onto the upper hall floor and then down the hall a bit. She made sure her boots clunked on the wooden floor as she returned to the stairs. Whistling, she came down the stairs, paintbox in hand.

"Good morning, Shan. Beautiful day, isn't it?" Harriet swept past the man without pausing.

He grunted in reply and moved deeper into the lodge. Harriet paused at the bottom of the outside steps to take a breath. So that was what that strange character and Shan had been up to in the dining room when what must have been money passed hands. It was really none of her affair, other than it was a sin, or so Father would say, to encourage any man to imbibe alcohol. The corner of her mouth tipped up. That phrase always amused her. As if a woman couldn't be tempted to get a bit tipsy. Harriet herself was more than a bit curious about what the attraction was. Maybe this summer she'd find out.

"I bet Winnie will be up to the challenge," she murmured before setting off toward the dock and her canoe. A quick survey of the area showed her that Tom and Winnie were nowhere in sight. So, either Tom appeased Winnie, or they'd gone their separate ways.

Even though the day was young yet, the sun beat down with a ferocity that promised stifling temperatures by the afternoon. Harriet set the paintbox down and flipped her canoe over, she placed the box securely under the bow seat before sliding the boat across the mud into the shallows. The pungent sent of hot, wet mud mixed with an undertone of decaying plant material rose around her as she pushed the canoe into deeper water before getting in. She leaned over and plucked a white water lily from the pads surrounding the craft. The sweet scent swirled around her as her paddle displaced the floating vegetation. The purple spikes of pickerelweed punctuated by the white of arrowhead weed brushed the sides of the canoe until she gained deeper water. Canoe Lake wasn't deep by some lake standards, the water by the Wapomeo islands was only thirty feet deep. Harriet grinned, which meant the water warmed earlier in the year than deeper lakes and made it perfect for swimming. She dipped her paddle into the still water, enjoying the pull of muscles across her back and shoulders. Kneeling as she was in the centre of the canoe, she had complete control and balance. When she'd first started canoeing last spring she'd perched on the rear seat which made her somewhat top heavy and her strokes less effective. Tom had taken pity on her one afternoon as she fought a stiff west wind with little success. Once he'd shown her how to kneel low in the canoe and in the centre rather than on the end, Harriet had been amazed at the difference it made.

Spying a lightning blasted spruce tree among some lower snags, she aimed the bow toward the spot. With the morning light streaming down like molten honey bringing out the variety of colours in the dead wood, it was just the subject she was looking for. The challenge of recreating the play of light and shadow and the striations in the twisted trunk had her fingers itching to pick up her brushes. Holding her anticipation in check she gave one last stroke and let the bow bump gently into the bit of sandy shore beneath the heap of granite rock the tree stood on. Moving carefully but quickly she hopped out and flipped the painter rope over a convenient bit of stump by the water's edge. Making sure her paddle was stowed, she picked up the paintbox and scrambled up the incline between two huge boulders. Gaining the vantage point she desired, Harriet opened the lid of the box and pulled out her materials. A sense of joy and soul healing peace settled over her. This was what life was about, living and breathing in the arms of nature and most of all doing what she loved. Smiling, she roughed in the outline she wanted before squeezing paint on her pallet and setting to work.

* * *

Hours later, tired, and more than a little sunburnt in spite of her long sleeves and hat pulled low over her face, Harriet packed up the morning's work. The light changed as the sun crossed the sky overhead and she lost the perspective she'd been chasing across her work. Massaging her stiff fingers, Harriet stood and stretched before looking at her easel with a critical eye. Head tipped to one side, she moved a foot to one side and then back. Yes, she decided, the bold strokes on the board captured the essence of the scene. This one might just be the one she converted to a larger canvas this winter. Either this one, or the birch grove. Indecision tugged at a corner of her mouth. Perhaps she would ask Tom what he thought and Winnie too. It never hurt to get other people's opinions, certainly those whose opinions she valued. She packed up her equipment and slid down the slope between the boulders landing in the wet sand by the canoe. It was only a moment's work to stow everything and unship the paddle.

The sun reflected off the water increasing the weight of the humidity that hung in the air. June in New Ontario could be a mixture of many things, rain, fog and unrelenting heat and humidity. Harriet pulled off her hat and ran her fingers through her sweat soaked hair, the cloth of her shirt sticking to her back.

"Lordy, lordy, it's hot," she murmured, plucking the shirt from her chest and flapping the material in a vain attempt to cool her heated skin. That was the trouble with getting so engrossed in her work, little things like bug bites and heat went undetected until she stopped. A quick glance up and down the lake confirmed there were no other boats in sight and the water by the big rocks was quite deep as the shore dropped off quickly.

After only a momentary hesitation Harriet shucked her sticky clothes, hanging the shirt and pants on a convenient bush to hopefully dry a bit before she had to get back into them. Shoving the socks into her heavy boots, she stood for a moment enjoying the soft breeze on her bare skin. Moving to the base of the boulders she stepped off the ledge and let the cool water close over her head. *What bliss!* She surfaced, blinking the water from her eyes. Treading water, she reached up and pulled the fastenings from her hair letting it float around her shoulders on the surface of the lake. Harriet flipped on her back and kicked her way out of the shadow of the bank, enjoying the combined feel of the water cooling her body and the sun on her face. Light sparkled though the water throwing ripples of light and shadow over her skin lying just below the surface. She closed her eyes and floated, letting the lake breath against her skin, sound deadened by the water covering her ears. This is what freedom feels like, she thought. No constrictions, no rules, well, other than keeping one's head above water. She grinned and flipped over onto her stomach, striking out further from the shore with smooth strong strokes.

Twenty minutes later, the sun started its descent toward the western trees and found Harriet clothed with her hair pilled haphazardly under hat headed back to Mowat Lodge. Safely tucked away were the results of the day's work. The stiffening breeze tugged at the stray strands of hair escaping from her hat. Harriet paused to tuck them behind her ears and then took up the rhythm of her stroke again. Beaching the canoe and stowing it, she strode up the trail to the lodge to find things in a turmoil.

* * *

Carrying her paintbox in one hand, with the paddle carelessly balanced on the other shoulder, Harriet hurried her step at the sound of raised voices.

"What's happening?" Harriet pulled Winnie away from the scrum of men gathered at the foot of the lodge steps.

"Some American looking for Martin Jr." Winnie kept her attention on Martin Bletcher Sr. who was gesticulating wildly, his face flushed bright red with agitation.

"Whatever for?" Harriet set the paintbox down by her feet and unshipped the paddle from her shoulder.

"It sounds like Martin Jr. came to Canada to avoid the conscription in the States. That tall man in the uniform is some sort of American military police sent to hunt him down." Winnie pointed to the man in the midst of the huddle of locals.

"And just where is Martin Jr.?" Harriet scanned the gathering.

Winnie snorted. "Probably hiding in a hole somewhere, the coward." She spat on the ground. "I can tell you Tom is steamed about it. You know he's tried to enlist twice, but they won't take him."

"I didn't realize that. Why are they rejecting him?"

"Flat feet," Winnie said. She glanced at her friend and confided. "I'm just as glad to tell you the truth. The thought of Tom being sent overseas and living in those trenches. I can tell you, if even half of the stories are true…" Winnie shuddered.

"I can't even imagine it," Harriet agreed. "What's going to happen with Bletcher Jr. though? Do you think that man is going to hang around hoping he'll show up?"

"I have no idea. I wouldn't put it past Tom to go out and hunt him down and drag him back here by the collar." Winnie glowered at Martin Sr. who was still pontificating at the top of the stairs.

"Where is Tom?" Harriet wondered aloud. "I don't see him in the crowd."

"He had a group of fishermen to guide today. I don't' expect him back until late this afternoon or early evening. Just as well for the Bletchers he's not here."

"Where's Bessie and Mrs. Blecher?"

"Oh no doubt Bessie is having vapours back at their cottage. I wouldn't be surprised is her useless brother isn't hiding under his mother's skirts."

"Now that's a picture, isn't it?" Harriet grinned.

"Coward, that's what he is. Personally, I think he sympathizes with the Germans and won't fight for the Allies." She turned her head away from the men and spoke into Harriet's ear. "There's been rumours about him spying for the enemy."

"How could he do that from out here in the bush?" Harriet frowned.

"Don't be silly, Harriet. Think how many trains go through here loaded with troops bound for Halifax? Bletcher Sr. has that radio thing he's always fooling with. What if it's not just an innocent hobby like he says?"

"I suppose," Harriet allowed. She had no liking for family, they were an elitist arrogant bunch in her opinion. Always acting like they were better than anyone else. "Well, if that is the case I hope they get caught and held accountable."

The two women moved back as the group of men began to break up. Martin Sr. disappeared into the gloom of the lodge with Shannon close behind. The American military policeman shook his head and mounted the horse he must have hired at the Canoe Lake train station. He turned the animal's head toward the men and fixed each one with a hard stare.

"If any of you know the whereabouts of Martin Bletcher Jr. you are obligated to report it to your military. We're all in this war together. Anyone neglecting to do their patriotic duty or worse still, spying for the enemy, deserves to be punished." With a last glare he kicked the horse around and headed down the trail.

"Well, that was a bit more excitement than I was expecting." Harriet picked up her paintbox and slung the paddle over her shoulder.

Winnie tagged along behind her when Harriet entered the lodge. Puzzled, Harriet made no comment as the other woman waited while she unlocked the door, then followed her inside and shut the door behind them.

"I need your advice, Harriet. I'm not sure what to do, but I think I need to do something."

"About what?" Harriet opened the paintbox to set her work out to cure in the light from the window. "Do you think Martin Jr. is actually spying for the Germans? Did you see something or hear something?

"Tom." Winnie ignored the questions concerning the American, sighed and plunked herself down on the bed, making the frame creak.

"Oh. What about him? Did you have a falling out?" Harriet settled on the one straight back wooden chair in the room.

"No, of course not. The opposite in fact." A slight flush rose up the woman's throat and across her cheeks. "We're engaged," she whispered.

"Why that's wonderful, isn't it. So, what's the issue?" Harriet struggled to follow the reasoning.

"The problem is he's reluctant to set a date and it's all Shan Fraser's fault!"

"How so?"

"Tom lent the Frasers two hundred and fifty dollars in order for them to buy some canoes and of course now that it's time to pay the money back they're coming up with all kinds of excuses and downright lies. I keep telling Tom he needs to be more forceful, demand his money back."

"What did he say about that?"

"He says he's asked both Shan and Annie for the money and they keep putting him off." Winnie got to her feet and paced across the room to glare out the window. "We need the money in order to pay for a honeymoon and Tom still needs to buy me a ring."

"Oh, no ring yet?" Harriet considered the situation. "When did you two come to an understanding?"

"Just this week. I mean we've been close for a long time and well now it's just imperative that it's made official."

"And why is that?" Harriet was getting an inkling of the situation.

Winnie continued to stare out the window, her back to Harriet. "I'm late."

The words were spoken so quietly Harriet wasn't sure she'd heard correctly. "I beg your pardon?"

Winnie swung back from the window. "I'm late," she repeated.

"You think you're carrying Tom's child? Are you sure? Perhaps you're just a bit late?"

"I'm fairly sure. I'm two weeks late and I'm always regular."

"Have you told him yet?"

"Of course! But I haven't told Father yet. I'm not sure that I will, at least not until I have a ring on my finger and hopefully a husband on my arm. You know an eight month child isn't unheard of for the first born. Please don't tell anyone. I can trust you to keep my secret, cant' I?"

"I won't tell a soul," Harriet promised. "What are you going to do if Tom can't get his money back?"

"We'll just have to get married without a ring or a honeymoon. I wish I had some money of my own like you do, but my father holds the purse strings, and he doesn't really approve of my relationship with Tom."

"Will Tom go along with that? You know who prickly some men are about their pride."

"He'll have to," Winnie insisted.

"I know it's not much help, but it you need to talk or a shoulder to cry on you know I'm here for you. Let's talk about something more pleasant for a moment. What plans do you have for Dominion Day?"

"I haven't really thought about it," Winnie confessed.

"Are you travelling back to Huntsville for the festivities or are you and your father staying at the cottage? I'm sure there will be some sort of do here. If nothing else it will be an excuse for the men to drink themselves stupid on that bootleg booze."

"I'm staying here, Father hasn't said one way or another what he is planning but I doubt he'll want to go to the bother and expense of returning home for just a couple of days."

"I'm glad then. I will at least have some female companionship other than Mrs. Fraser." Harriet took Winnie's hands in hers. "I'm sure it will all work out in the end. Tom is a good man, I'm sure he'll stand behind you and marry you."

"He better." Winnie managed a watery smile.

"You don't have doubts, do you?" Harriet frowned.

The other woman shook her head. "Not really, I'm just anxious to get it settled, before...well you know..." She ran her hand over her still flat belly.

Chapter Six

Dominion Day dawned hazy and hot. The mist was still dancing on the lake when Harriet opened her curtains on the narrow window. Even at six-thirty in the morning the heat was rising from the swampy earth by the water's edge and the sun struck hot through the single pane glass. She considered going back to bed for a lie in, but decided against it as the heat and humidity would soon make such an endeavour uncomfortable.

Instead, Harriet tipped the tepid water from the ceramic pitcher into the basin on the dresser and gave herself a quick wash. With any luck there would be time for a swim later on. In fact, she promised herself she'd make sure there was time. Pulling on a light cambric men's shirt and her canvas trousers, she considered going barefoot but pulled on socks and stamped her feet into her boots. She could always shuck the boots and socks once she was out on the water.

Paintbox in hand and paddle over her shoulder, she locked her door and headed toward the welcome scent of coffee wafting up the stairs. Setting her belongings at a vacant table, she sauntered over to the coffee urn. From the corner of her vision, she noticed Winnie and Tom sitting by the window, heads close together. She caught Winnie's eye and gave a quick wave, but didn't intrude on the couple. Sitting down, she drank the coffee slowly, while contemplating putting together a bit of a lunch from the meagre breakfast offerings to take with her out on the lake. A quick glance told her neither of the Frasers were present at the moment. Pulling her kerchief from her pocket, Harriet went to the sideboard and gathered up some biscuits, cheese, onions, and pickles. There was a few stringy bits of bacon lying forlornly on a greasy plate which she passed on. She stuffed the laden kerchief into the front of her shirt, gathered up her things and escaped before either Fraser could demand payment for her lunch.

The bright sunlight caused her to pause on the top step to allow her eyes to adjust. Then, with a light step, she hopped down the stairs and headed for her canoe and the solitude of the lake. It would be just about perfect if the Blechers didn't come nosing around in their little motor craft, disturbing the peace, and setting the jays and other birds into an uproar. Martin Jr. gave her the willies with the way he looked at her and Martin Sr. wasn't much better in her opinion. Even quiet, sallow Betsy was a strange bird, always keeping to herself and within close range of her family. It was

61

actually a blessing that the younger Blecher had gone into hiding. No doubt he'd show up tonight, not being one to miss out on the booze.

Harriet shrugged and pushed the thought away as she slid the canoe into the shallows until it was deep enough for her to step in. Settling the folded canvas to cushion her knees from the ribs of the cedarstrip and stowing the paintbox safely under the bow seat Harriet paddled away from the dock. The sweet scent of the white lilies she disturbed with her efforts rose in the humid air to envelop her. She smiled, now if only someone could bottle that and sell it as perfume...it would be like capturing summer to release in a mist in the midst of winter.

"How anyone could do that is beyond my ken," she said out loud, borrowing the Scottish word from her mother. The lake was fairly smooth, but an east wind was blowing as she came out from behind the Wapomeo islands. Perhaps Tea Lake Dam was a bit ambitious for how she was feeling. Instead, she moved closer to the shoreline with an eye out for a likely place to beach the canoe and have a wander in the bush. With the July sun working its way to the zenith, the play of golden light and shadow through the pale green leaves would pick out the browns, russets and reds of last year's leaves carpeting the ground under the trees and if she was very lucky she would find some lady's slippers and hopefully a riot of trilliums gathered around the trunks. Time would tell. She grinned and hummed as she paddled.

* * *

The sun was hovering just over the treeline by the time Harriet beached her canoe and made her way toward the lodge. She hummed as she walked, paintbox swinging in her hand and paddle shipped on her shoulder. The day had been glorious, three new paintings were safely stowed in her box, the solitude and beauty of the time spent in communication with the lake and bush were a source of joy and contentment in her heart.

Nearing the lodge, she took in the scene of chaos. Trestle tables were set out and a large area cleared for the bonfire. Annie was bustling about, her shrill voice shouting orders and abuse to the men attempting to do her bidding. Harriet slipped by the area and entered the building. She sorely needed to change her clothes and take a quick sponge bath to rid herself of the sweat of the day. Not to mention getting the pigments off her fingers and from under her nails.

"Harriet! There you are. I was afraid you'd decided to go to Sprucedale for the festivities after all." Winnie met her on the way up the stairs.

"Not at all. I was just enjoying a day in the bush." She held up her paintbox. "A very productive day."

"Well, hurry and put your things away. Annie's after commandeering everyone to help with things." Winnie skipped down the stairs, then turned. "Oh, I almost forgot. Annie was looking for you earlier. Said there was a letter or a telegram for you."

Harriet frowned. "That's odd. I can't imagine who would be contacting me. There wouldn't have been mail delivery to the station today, anyway."

Winnie shrugged. "You know how it goes. Might have come yesterday when Shannon went down to Canoe station…"

"Oh, I've been warned, never fear. I'm well aware of the Frasers' penchant for reading other people's mail. I'll ask her about it later." Harriet's gaze followed Winnie's passage down the stairs, a frown creasing her forehead. No point worrying about it right now, she reasoned. If it was something worrisome she'd find out soon enough.

Twenty minutes later, Harriet bounded down the stairs, hair freshly washed and tied back from her face, the clean clothes rustling pleasantly as she moved. The thought of good food and festivities around the fire put a spring in her step. She enjoyed the informal gatherings at Mowat to the more formal and regimented goings on her father would preside over at home. Spying Winnie, she joined her in moving some benches over by the firepit.

"Where's Tom today?"

"Around here somewhere." Winnie glanced over her shoulder and lowered her voice. "He's planning to ask Shannon for the money he's owed today. He told me he's made arrangements for a honeymoon cottage at Billy Bear Lodge."

"That's good news, then. You must be happy about that."

"I am, yes. But I'm also concerned. He heard about that American coming to look for Blecher Jr, and he's got his blood up about that. It was all I could do this morning to stop him for storming over to their cottage and calling the man out for avoiding the conscription."

"I suppose I can understand that. From things Tom's let drop in conversation I know he's upset about getting refused for military duty."

Winnie nodded. "He feels guilty for being here at home and safe while so many young men are overseas risking their lives. The list of missing and dead in the papers just eats at his soul."

"It's not like he hasn't tried to enlist twice. He really has nothing to feel guilty about, but then I'm not a man, so maybe I just don't understand the need to go become a target."

"Honestly, I'm relieved he isn't being sent overseas. Especially now". Winnie smoothed her skirts over a still flat belly.

"You still haven't got your monthlies, then?" Harriet rolled a flat topped stump into the ring of seats by the fire pit.

"No. I'm pretty sure I'm with child."

"Have you told Tom yet?"

"Tonight. I figure to once he's spoken with Shan and made arrangements to get his money. Then I'll tell him. I know he'll be thrilled."

"I'm sure he will," Harriet assured her, even though she herself wasn't so sure.

* * *

Sunlight poured in streams of golden-honey light across Canoe Lake touching everything in its path with a sense of magic. At least that was Harriet's thought as she climbed the steps of the lodge. Everything was arranged and it was time to clean up and change into something not wet with sweat. The approaching July evening promised to be as hot and humid as the day had been. With any luck a breeze would come in from the west and provide a bit of cooling. The seductive scent of the roast pig followed her into the lodge. The hog had been roasting since the morning and the smell of the fat dripping into the pit and sizzling almost drove Harriet mad. With thoughts of the festivities to come, she hurried toward the stairs.

"Harriet!" Annie Fraser's summons stopped her with one foot on the bottom riser.

With a sigh, she turned and crossed the hall to the office door. "Did you need me for something?"

"No, no." Annie held out a somewhat tattered envelope. "This came for you, and I thought you would want to see it as soon as possible."

Harriet took the proffered envelope. "Thank you. I didn't know Shan went into the station this morning." Her fingers tested the seal of the envelope flap.

Annie met her gaze squarely, a smugness hiding in her expression, there and then gone so soon Harriet thought she might have imagined it if she hadn't known better.

"He brought it back late last night when he came in with the hog. I expect you must have already gone to bed. Didn't want to disturb you." Annie busied herself straightening some papers on her desk, then got to her feet. "'Scuse me, I need to start setting out the rest of the food. People'll be arriving before I know it."

Harriet stepped back and let her pass, tucking the envelope in her pocket. Crossing the hall, she took the steps two at a time. Once in her room with the door securely locked, she pulled the letter out and examined it more closely. It was hard to tell but she was fairly sure the flap had been steamed and resealed. A valid assumption based on her knowledge of the inn keepers and the warnings she'd had from both Tom and Winnie. No matter, she decided, it couldn't be anything too important as the copperplate handwriting was her father's. She sat on the edge of the bed and slit the envelope open.

Monday June 25, 1917
Dear Daughter,
I write to you with happy news. As you will no doubt recall our conversation before you left for the bush country, you will also recall that I broached the issue of your as yet unmarried state. A woman of your age is considered a spinster in polite society, and your mother and I despair for you. With that in mind, I have taken the necessary steps to remedy the situation."

Harriet blinked and read the first paragraph again, her jaw tense and a hard knot in her stomach. "How dare he?" she hissed. "How dare he? Does he think he can sell me to the highest bidder like a prize broodmare?" Taking a deep breath, she read on.

I realize you have sequestered yourself at that rundown lodge operated by those odious people and I have no chance of persuading you to come home to Sprucedale. With that in mind, I have taken the liberty of interviewing prospective husbands for you, and I am pleased to say I have, with consultation with your mother, chosen a man who I believe will be able to keep your wayward tendencies in line.

As aforementioned, I acknowledge your stubbornness and female hysteria in insisting on spending so much time away from polite society, so I, accompanied by your fiancé intend to arrive at Canoe Lake train station on the afternoon of July 4, 1917. You do not need to worry about arranging transportation for us from the station to your lodge as I have contacted the Thomases who operate the train station and they have informed me they are invited to the Dominion Day festivities at Mowat Lodge and will gladly give us transport.

I trust this finds with your approval and I look forward to introducing you to your future husband.

Your father,
Baldwin Ivan St. George
Sprucedale, Ontario

"Damn, damn, damn." Harriet lurched to her feet, crumpling the letter in her hand. What in the name of God was she supposed to do now? "There is now way in hell I'm agreeing to marry some man I've never even met, no matter what Father has promised

69

him." She took a deep, steadying breath. "I'll just refuse to go along with this insanity. I am of legal age and I have a secure income which he cannot touch, and I'll be damned if some man Father has handpicked to take me off his hands will ever see a penny of it. Thank God Aunt Lois put all those provisions in her bequest." She paced around the room, pausing to toss the cursed letter onto her dresser. "I will just refuse, he can't make me do anything. He's just going to have to see that and then he can explain it to whoever this man is." She nodded firmly. "Yes, that's how it will happen. Father will have to see reason."

Still fuming, she washed quickly and changed into clean clothes. Stepping into the hall, she met Winnie coming from her room.

"All set?" Winnie beamed at her. "Tom is back from Tea Lake Dam, and he's promised to ask Shan for the money."

"That's nice," Harriet muttered, nervous thoughts still circling in her mind.

"What's the matter?" Winnie took her arm. "Did something happen? Was it that letter Annie was on about?"

"Oh, yes. Definitely the letter. It's from my father, and he's planning on showing up here today."

"Whatever for?" Winnie frowned. "Is there trouble at home he's come to tell you about? Some sickness perhaps?"

"Oh, there's trouble all right, but not at home. Father," she bit the word off, "has decided that I need to be married and he's on his way here with his chosen candidate for my hand."

"Oh, my! No wonder Annie looked so smug when she told me there was a letter for you. What are you going to do? Surely you don't intend to marry this man?" Winnie grasped her hand. "Is there anything I can do to help you? You're welcome to hide out at the cottage..."

"Thank you, but that shouldn't be necessary. I will just explain to Father that there is no way I will agree to whatever arrangements he has made. And that should be that."

"How can you be so sure? For him to make the journey up here, and on a holiday at that, he must be certain of his success. Wouldn't it be better if you just weren't around when he gets here?"

Harriet shook her head. "I'm not afraid of him and I refuse to run away like a wayward child. I'm a grown woman, quite capable of surviving on my own without a man to *guide* me. Come, let's go down and join the crowd." She led the way down the stairs and out into the clearing by the fire.

Winnie followed her, biting her lip. Fathers could be so unpredictable and troublesome at times. While her father might have heard about Winnie's attachment to Tom Thomson, she hadn't had the courage to broach the subject of her engagement with him yet. Let alone that she feared she was with child. She shuddered; she could only imagine what his reaction to *that* would be. Time enough to worry about that later. Tonight, she intended to have a good time and if need be run interference for Harriet with her father.

The two women stepped out into the gathering dusk and made their way toward the fire where the smoke chased away the clouds of mosquitoes and biting insects.

Chapter Seven

Harriet joined the group of people by the fire. Bats swooped around the eves of the lodge and the first stars popped out of the deep velvet blue of the evening sky. A quick glance told her that Father and whoever he was bringing weren't by the fire. But then neither was Shannon, he might at this very moment be driving back from the train station with his passengers bouncing against the sides of his makeshift carriage. A grim smile twisted her lips at the thought of how Father would react to that.

A pine log in the fire burst in a brilliant spray of sparks, flames blooming like a wavering flower from the height of the blaze. Someone brought out a guitar and another man started tuning a fiddle. Soon the night rang with voices raised in somewhat harmonious song. The quality of the music didn't matter to Harriet, it was just a joy to part of the boisterous community. Her voice choked off in mid-song when a large hand gripped her shoulder.

"Daughter, I would have a word with you." Baldwin St. George hauled her to her feet. "In private." He glared at Winnie who had risen to her feet as well.

"Do you want me to come with you?" Winnie ignored the man and spoke directly to Harriet.

"I'll be fine. Don't worry." Harriet's words were almost drowned out by her father.

"It is of little matter what Miss St. George wants or does not want. It is my word that is law."

Harriet shook her head at Winnie to dissuade her from further protestations. When Father was in this mood it was best to tread carefully and make careful plans for an escape at the first possibility. She allowed her father to tow her toward the lamp lit lodge door where she noticed the tall figure of a man silhouetted against the light. She bit her lip, most likely her erstwhile suiter. The toe of her boot caught on the top step in her hurry to keep up with her father's longer stride. Mentally cursing her clumsiness, she pulled her shoulders back and shrugged off the hand on her arm.

"Miss St. George." The tall man swept off his hat and bent his head in a facsimile of a bow.

Harriet tipped her head back and glared at the man, noticing the balding spot on the top of his head. "And who do I have the pleasure of speaking with?" she kept her tone cold and formal while somehow allowing it to drip with contempt.

Father stepped forward. "Allow me to introduce my daughter, Miss Harriet Agnes St. George. Harriet, this is Wendal Henry Featherswallow, The third."

"Your servant, m'am." He reached for her hand.

"Pleased, I'm sure." Harriet shoved both hands into the pockets of her trousers.

Father glared at her, and she glared back. Nothing on this green earth was going to make her encourage this nonsense and the harder she made it for both men the better.

"I fear I am at a loss, Miss St. George. I was given to believe that you were in accord with the arrangements between myself and your father."

The man looked sincere, but Harriet hardened her heart against him. "I fear you are very much mistaken, Mr. Featherswallow. I have no wish to be wed to you or in fact to anyone. I apologize that my father has dragged you out here under false pretenses." She turned to go back down the steps.

"Actually, Miss St. George, it is you who are labouring under false pretenses. There has been a contract signed and money exchanged, under the law you are now my property, or chattel, if you prefer that wording."

Harriet rounded on her father who actually took a step backward from her fury. "You must be joking, Father. You have no right to do such a thing."

"In the eyes of the law, he does," Featherswallow broke in, "you are an unmarried spinster and living in your father's house. He is responsible for you and has taken steps to see you are well taken care of. You see, I am a lawyer, and I assure you what has passed between your father and myself is perfectly legal and will stand up in court of law." He replaced his hat and rather pompously tucked his hand into the front of his waistcoat.

"We shall see about that. I have a lawyer of my own and will be contacting him by telegram tomorrow morning. In the meantime, I suggest you see if Mrs. Fraser has rooms for you as I have no intention of sharing mine. Now, if you will excuse me I will rejoin the party and celebrate Dominion Day." She swept down the stairs with as much grace and dignity as one could clad in heavy boots, a flannel shirt, and trousers. All in all, Harriet thought she managed it with some style. She left the two men in the doorway of the lodge gaping after her. Her mind whirled with possibilities, if there was any truth in what Featherswallow said she might be in trouble. What kind of name was that anyway? She shivered vowing it would never be hers. It didn't take any imagination to see that Father was bent on this line of action. A cold chill raised the hair on the nape of her neck when she remembered how the man had his sister admitted to an insane asylum when she refused to do his bidding.

Sadly, it was easy enough to commit someone, especially a woman who many men in the medical profession claimed were prone to hysteria and posed a danger to themselves and others. "Think again if you are entertaining any idea of that," she growled. Discretion might be the better part of valour however, she decided as she rejoined Winnie by the trestle tables of food. It might be best if she slipped away tonight after everything was quiet. She was perfectly capable of surviving in the bush for a couple of weeks as long as the weather held. Surely Father would grow tired of living in the squalor he certainly viewed the lodge of providing.

"Winnie, I need your help," she whispered while piling a tin plate with food. "I think I'm in trouble."

"What do you need, my friend. Is that man the one your father has chosen for you?" She tipped her head toward the man following Baldwin toward the fire.

Harriet nodded. "He's a lawyer and claims he's basically bought me from Father. For my own good, of course."

"Hog wash," Winie spit the word out. "Laws regarding women have to change and soon. What are you planning?"

"I was going to contact my own lawyer in the morning, but then I remembered how Father committed his younger sister to an insane asylum when she refused to do as he bid. I wouldn't put it past him to do the same to me. Just to save face and salve his pride in the view of his *polite society.*"

"Oh my word, that's terrible. What are you going to do?" Winnie led the way to a couple of empty seats just within the ring of fire light.

"I believe it would be prudent for me to disappear tonight after things quiet down. I have my canoe and if I can borrow Tom's tent I should be quite fine for a few days."

"No need to ask, I can get the tent for you. I'll get together a basket of food that won't spoil, and I know you can fish quite well so you shouldn't go hungry. Where are you planning to flee to?"

"I'm not sure yet, and it's best you don't know too much, or Father will find a way to get it out of you. Trust me, he can be relentless."

"I call you a coward and a deserter," Tom's voice cut through the babble of voices.

Harriet and Winnie both stood and moved toward the side of the fire where Tom Thomson and Martin Blecher Jr. were nose to nose.

"You're a coward yourself, Thomson. I don't see you in uniform and squatting in the lice ridden trenches." Blecher shot a hand out and shoved the other man hard in the shoulder.

"Bastard! German sympathizing bastard." Tom doubled his fist and hit Blecher in the face.

The other man stumbled backward and came back swinging his fists wildly. The two men circled each other exchanging insults and occasionally landing blows. Finally, one of Thomson's fists connected soundly with the other man's chin and he went down in a shower of dust.

"Enough, that is enough," Martin Blecher Sr. strode forward to help his son to his feet. "Come Bessie, Louisa, it is time we were going." He dragged his son into the darkness, followed by his daughter and wife.

"This isn't over, Thomson. You better watch your back, you bastard," Martin Jr.'s voice came out of the dark.

Tom rubbed a hand over his mouth and accepted a mug of spirits from Mark Robinson. After a moment of awkward silence, broken only by the crackling of the fire, someone struck up a tune on the fiddle and soon everyone was singing again. Harriet warily kept track of her father and Featherswallow on the far side of the ring of light. It was worrying that Father seemed to have Shannon's ear and she was fairly certain that money changed hands between the two. What was that about? Surely, it didn't bode well for Harriet, of that she was sure.

"Winnie says you have need of my tent for a while," Tom said at her elbow, diverting her attention from the conclave of men across the fire.

"I do, as long as you are willing and able to keep my secret." Harriet looked up at him.

"Aye, Winnie's told me your trouble. You're welcome to the tent and anything else you may need. I'd be furious if my father treated my sisters in such a way."

"Thank you, Tom. It means a lot, your assistance. I fear I must make my escape this evening as I mislike the way Father is cozied up with Shan."

Tom glanced across the fire and nodded. "An unholy union if ever I saw one." He grinned.

Winnie giggled and leaned against him. "I'm off to go and pilfer some food supplies for Harriet. If you can bring the tent to the cottage as soon as you can without raising suspicion, Harriet can slip out and paddle over there so we can load up the canoe." She raised herself on tiptoe and kissed his cheek before disappearing into the gloom beyond the fire light.

"You're sure you'll be okay by yourself out in the bush, Hetty?" Firelight threw shadows across his rugged features, one cheek darkening with a bruise from his recent fisticuffs.

"I'll be fine. Anything is better than being shackled to a man I don't even know." She shuddered. "Thank you again for your assistance." She paused. "Has Winnie spoken to you about setting a date for the wedding?"

"She has," Tom was terse. "I'm at a loss to figure out why she's in such a hurry. Do you have any idea?"

Ah, so Winnie hasn't told him about the pregnancy yet. Harriet shook her head. "That's a conversation you need to have with Winnie. My advice to you is not to wait too much longer or matters may be taken out of your hands."

"Now that's as enigmatic as speech as I've heard in a long time, though I take your meaning to heart." He straightened his shoulders. "I suppose I must go beard the lion in his den and persuade Fraser to repay me the money I loaned him this spring." He sighed and squeezed Harriet's arm. "Be careful, Hetty. Promise me."

"I will, of course. And good luck with Shan."

Tom snorted. "I'll need it." He left her strode around the fire, effectively breaking up whatever tete a tete Father was having with Shannon.

The night was wearing on and the number of the people left at the gathering were mostly men who had indulged in too much moonshine. Harriet made her escape into the friendly dark and headed toward the lodge door.

"Retiring so soon?" Featherswallow loomed out of the night, between her and her destination.

"I find I am tired from all the excitement. I intend to retire to my room." She attempted to step around him.

"A wise choice, perhaps all is not lost with you. I would caution you to remain in your room and lock the door. Any attempt to leave your room will end most unfortunately for you I am afraid. It would be construed as female hysteria, lurking around in the dark, most unfortunate, if you catch my drift.

"Be sure that I do." Harriet pushed by him.

"I stopped by to see that your Aunt Matilda was being well cared for at the Muskoka Cottage Sanitorium. Such a sad place and such a pity to see the inhabitants incarcerated there."

"And how is she?" Harriet couldn't help stopping to ask. Aunt Matilda has always been kind to her.

"Oh, you know, the same. Quite drugged to keep her happy." Featherswallow shrugged.

Harriet turned back toward him. "My aunt is no more insane than you are. I suppose it was you who helped Father put her away." Her breath hissed between clenched teeth.

"He enlisted my assistance, yes." He gripped her chin in his fingers and tilted her head up. "Marry me as your father wishes and be sure the same thing doesn't happen to you."

She jerked her head away and glared at him. Without another word she rounded on her heel and stamped into the lodge. Once on the broad stairs and out of his sight, she stopped and gripped the railing, fighting to control her rage and her ragged breathing.

"As if I would ever marry a cold fish like that," she whispered. "I'd drown myself in the lake first. I bet Father hasn't thought of that possibility. He doesn't know me at all."

She continued up to her room where she shut and locked the door and for good measure drew the dresser over in front of it. Quickly she packed what she thought she would need and opened the window so she could hear when the revelry died down.

* * *

Harriet turned the lamp out to discourage moths and insects from coming in through the open window. She was just drowsing off when raised voices roused her. Throwing back the light covering, she padded to the window.

"Like hell I still owe you anything," Shannon Fraser's voice was loud and belligerent with drink. The flames of the fire lit his face with an unholy glow.

"You bloody well do owe me, and you know it," Tom Thomson shouted back, also a little worse for the drink. "I need that money now."

"No way I've got that kind of cash lying around," Shannon prevaricated.

"By the end of the week then, or next Monday by the latest."

Shannon made some comment too low to carry to Harriet's window. Whatever it was he said, Tom swung around and landed a right hook on the man's chin, followed by an uppercut to the gut. Fraser reared back and hit Tom in the head with the jug in his hand. Tom staggered back but didn't go down.

"This isn't finished, Fraser. Monday at the latest." Tom let Winnie drag him away out of the light of the fire. Presumably to tend to any wounds and to put an end to the quarrel.

"Good luck to you both," Harriet muttered and returned to bed.

By two-thirty in the morning the fire was burning down to ashes. Harriet lurked by the window until the fire was well wetted down and put out. It appeared everyone had retired. Footsteps echoed outside her door and the handle rattled.

"There...locked from the outside. There's no way the chit can get out," Featherswallow's voice was muffled by the door.

"The girl will come around, you will see. Females do not know their own minds or what's good for their welfare," Father's voice faded as the two men continued on down the hall.

Harriet counted to one-hundred and then moved on silent feet to try the door.

"Bother and damn," she cursed. Though she released the lock from her side of the door it refused to budge. "No matter. There's more than one way to skin a cat."

Gathering up the items she'd packed earlier and her paintbox, she forced the window sash up as far it would go. After a quick look to be sure no one was lurking under the window in the shadows of the lodge, she lowered her belongings out the window and down to the ground with a spare painter line from the docks. Then, securing the line to the bedstead she clambered out the window, balancing on the sill and listening for any indication someone was about. Satisfied she was alone Harriet rappelled down the side of the building with as little noise as possible. Once her feet hit the ground she collected her items and hiked into the darkness.

By the time she reached the canoe her breath was short in her chest. Stowing her baggage, she pushed the canoe into deeper water and set out across the star spangled lake. Thank goodness there was only a waning moon tonight and no real moonlight to betray her. In a matter of minutes that seemed like hours, the canoe bumped gently against the Trainor's dock. Reluctant to leave the vessel, Harriet put hand on the cleat nearest her and peered into the dark.

"Hetty, is that you?" Tom's voice floated out of the gloom.

"Yes," she hissed. "Did you bring the tent?"

Two figures appeared at the end of the dock, the darkened cottage behind them.

"Father is asleep, but we need to be quiet. He's a light sleeper," Winnie whispered, handing Harriet a bundle which she stowed in the canoe.

"Here's the tent and a few other things I thought you might find useful," Tom said.

Harriet took the proffered equipment with hands that shook a little. "Thanks, you two. I hope I don't get you into any hot water over this. Father can be rather nasty when he's crossed."

"Let us worry about that. Best you get yourself gone." Tom gave the canoe a slight shove away from the dock. "Be careful."

"I will," she whispered and stuck out with the paddle. In moments the dock and cottage disappeared into the night and Harriet was alone with the black velvet lake and sable sky. A sense of peace descended on her, as it always did when she was on the water. Getting her bearings from the hulking shapes of the two Wapomeo Islands, she turned the bow of the canoe toward the tiny, secluded cove she'd scouted out. It was a place she often went to paint, but not one she'd shared with anyone, including Tom.

Now she was glad of that fact. Even if Father threatened and pushed for information, neither of her friends knew about the place. With a grim smile, she slipped the paddle into the still water and set out for freedom and adventure.

Chapter Eight

The stars swirled and scattered across the water where the paddle disturbed their reflection. Harriet thought six days should be more than enough time for Father's patience to wear thin. With any luck he and Featherswallow were safely back in Sprucedale or Huntsville or God willing Featherswallow would be back in England. Faint illumination that dimmed the stars heralded the approach of dawn on this seventh day of July 1917. She allowed the canoe to drift in silence, hugging the shoreline as she approached the vantage point she'd selected to see if Winnie's signal of safe return was visible. As the sky brightened, the red scarf tied to the upright post of the Trainor dock shone through the mist rising from the dark waters.

"Perfect," she whispered and dipped the paddle into the lake. "Now as long as the Frasers haven't rented my room while I've been absent, all will be well."

After stowing the canoe, Harriet hiked up to the lodge with her belongings. The day was humid even at this early hour with the promise of a hot day ahead. She paused in the hall just inside the door of the lodge to wipe the sweat from her face, setting her gear down by her feet.

"Well, well. It's about time you showed up." Shannon Fraser regarded her from the door of the dining room.

"I've just been out in the bush painting. Nothing unusual in that." Harriet picked up her gear and moved toward the stairs.

Shannon snorted. "Not the tale I heard. Running off in the middle of the night." He shook his head. "Your father and that dandy with him were right pissed off."

"That's no concern of yours." Harriet looked down her nose at him, giving a good impression of her mother's haughty look which worked so well on the servants. She hoped she succeeded as it never worked quite so well for Harriet as it did for her mother.

"Is that Harriet?" Annie appeared in the door of her cubby hole office.

"Yup, the return of the prodigal," Shannon replied, a sardonic grin on his face.

"Is my room unlocked?" Harriet put on foot on the first riser.

"New door it's got." Annie nodded.

"Whatever for? The old door was quite adequate." Harriet frowned.

"That it was, until your intended broke it down. Lucky for you they didn't harm the furniture you had shoved in front of it."

"They broke the door down?" Harriet was flabbergasted, although on reflection, violence wasn't outside Father's predilections, and it appeared the man he'd chosen to sell her to was of the same disposition. A lucky escape on her part. A thought occurred to her. "And I suppose I'm liable for the cost of replacement?" She tapped her booted foot.

A sly smile crossed Shannon's face, before Annie spoke over him. "Oh no. We insisted on payment before they got a ride to the station." She chuckled. "Not like those two were going to walk there." Shannon glowered at his wife, annoyed he'd missed the possibility to be paid twice for the damage, Harriet supposed.

"Well, that's a relief, then. I'll just go on up and get settled." She went up the stairs.

"Oh, I almost forgot." Annie's voice halted her partway up the steps. "There came a telegram for you two, maybe three, days ago."

Sighing, Harriet continued to the landing and set her gear down before going back down to retrieve the telegram from Annie's fingers.

"I suppose you know what's in here?" She raised an eyebrow at the stout, shorter woman.

"Of course I don't!" Annie jammed her hands in belligerence on her ample hips. "What are you accusing me of?"

"Nothing, of course. It's just the seal on the flap has been tampered with."

"Weren't us," Shannon broke in. "Might 'a bin the young fella Thomas sent up with it."

"I'll be sure to mention it to Mister Thomas next time I see him." Giving up the argument, Harriet retrieved her belongings and went along the hall to her room. Once she was settled, the first thing she would do was find Winnie and let her know she was back and safe. Stowing her few items, she sank onto the side of the bed and opened the telegram with its Great North Western Telegram logo printed boldly across the top. It wasn't from Father as she'd expected, but from his attorney.

Huntsville, Ontario July 4, 1917
Miss Harriet Agnes St. George
Re your actions of July 1 1917. I been notified by my client Baldwin St. George to inform you that as of the above date all ties to the family of Baldwin St. George and any subsequent descendants have been severed. In Mr. St George's words, "Harriet Agnes St. George is no longer recognized as a member of this family, immediate and all related branches of said family. I disown and disinherit her."

Signed this 4th day of July it the year of our Lord 1917 in the village of Huntsville Ontario
George Summerville Wilgress
Attorney at Law
Huntsville, Ontario

Harriet read it over three times before folding it and tucking it into her pocket. Emotions coursed through her and she was at a loss to put a name to most of them. Anger, confusion, to name a few, and sorrow underlying them all. Disowned. Never to see the home she'd grown up in, never to speak to Amelia, her favourite sister, again. She blinked back the tears that threatened and straightened her back. Disowned she might be, but she was still her own woman, and best of all, free of Father's machinations to see her married to a suitable gentleman. Dear Lord! Featherswallow? An English fop if ever she'd seen one, no doubt he'd expected her to just up and move to England with him. Small chance of that, and now, well now...she was free. She collapsed onto the quilt and shut her eyes, thoughts milling around in her mind. Before she realized it, the nights spent sleeping rough in the bush caught up with her and in spite of her best intentions to seek out Winnie and hopefully Tom, she fell asleep.

* * *

A tap on the door brought Harriet out of her slumber, rubbing her eyes, and pulling down the shirt which had ridden up her midriff while she slept, she stumbled across and opened the door.

"Thank God you're safe!" Winnie burst through the door, kicking it shut behind her before hugging Harriet.

"Yes, yes, I'm fine. I must have fallen asleep. I meant to come and find you right after I got back."

"I came as soon as I heard. Shan was talking with Mark Robinson and I overheard you name." She grasped Harriet's hands. "It's such a shame about your father. How could he do such a thing? It's a disgrace, that's what it is."

"Whatever are you talking about?" Harriet prevaricated, but was fairly sure the news of contents of the telegram in her pocket was feeding the gossip mill of Mowat.

Winnie had the grace to blush and drop her gaze. "I'm that sorry. I suppose you would have preferred to keep that private," she shrugged, "but you know what things are around here."

"Sadly, I do. No matter, Winnie. People would have found out at any rate. It's just rather annoying that the Frasers feel they have the right to be privy to their guests' private correspondence. Does Tom know?"

Winnie nodded. "He's the one who told me."

Harriet snorted. "I suppose he heard it from Shannon?"

The other woman glanced away. "Actually, Tom heard it from Mark, who overheard Annie telling Mrs. Thomas from the station."

"Isn't that just wonderful? Everyone in the vicinity has heard about it before me." In spite of herself Harriet laughed. "Doesn't that just beat all? I imagine Father would be furious if he knew his business was spread all over the place."

"What are you going to do?"

"What do you mean? I have my own means of support." Harriet hesitated. "Though I suppose I will have to find a house to rent, preferably in Huntsville. I can't imagine living in Sprucedale in such close proximity to the family. In a pinch I could maybe get one of the Dean's cottages on Doe Lake, but I'd rather not do that."

"Oh, yes!" Winnie clapped her hands. "Do come to Huntsville, Harriet. It will be so nice to have a friend so close."

"Time to worry about that once September comes. Now, tell me have you told Tom about...you know..." Harriet nodded towards Winnie's waist.

"I did."

"How did he take it?"

"He wasn't thrilled, but it's going to be all right. We're going to be married, but there is one small problem."

"What's that?" Harriet frowned.

"Tom wants to go west and paint mountains. His friend came back recently full of raptures about his experience in the Rockies."

"Couldn't you go with him after you're married? Providing you got married soon."

"We did talk about that, but nothing is decided yet. Are you planning on trying to talk with your father about all this?" Winnie waved a hand toward the telegram Harriet had pulled from her pocket.

"Not a chance. In retrospect this break has been coming for a long time, I had always hoped that we might make the break amicably. Although knowing Father, I do believe I was being overly optimistic. No. I will go on living my life as I see fit, and now, without the burden of the family's disapproval of my actions." She got to her feet and pulled Winnie up with her. "Let's go find Tom and see if we can persuade him to firm things up with you. At the very least set a date so you and I can make some arrangements."

The two women left the room giggling, pattered down the steps and out of the lodge.

* * *

The following morning dawned a bit overcast with a light rain falling intermittently. Harriet decided to hike into the bush in search of interesting locations to come back to later and paint. She had no wish to attempt to put oil to board in the inclement weather, but perhaps it would turn sunny later. Setting out toward the Joe Lake portage she ran into Tom and Shan returning from some business they had with the Algonquin Lodge.

"Good morning, gentlemen," she greeted them.

"Morning," Tom drawled while Shannon nodded his grizzly head.

"Any luck with that big fish you men are always angling for? Anyone win the bet yet?" Harriet tipped her head back and grinned.

"No luck," Tom confessed. "Although, I think I will go over to Tea Lake and maybe beyond. See if I can catch one big enough to fool Mark. I'd dearly love to put one over on him." Laugh lines crinkled at the corners of his eyes.

"I'll never tell," Shannon promised. "But come over to the lodge and get some provisions, just in case it takes a couple of days."

"I'll do that. Bye, Hetty. Be careful on your own in the bush." Tom shouldered his fishing rod, shifting the wicker creel to his other hand. The two men disappeared down the trail until the bush hid them from view.

Harriet struck out along the north side of the lake, keeping to the higher ground. Somewhere nearby there was a hollow with a small stream running through it and a tiny pond which she wanted to relocate. She'd found it early in the year on one of her rambles and was fairly sure she could find it again. Maybe.

Forty minutes later she was no wiser as to where her hollow was hiding. Harriet turned toward where she knew the lake lay hidden by trees surmounting a low ridge. The sound of voices told her she was close to the shore. Gripping a sapling for support, she gained the top of the rise and looked down between the trunks at the glimmer of Canoe Lake. The voices came again, faint and carried on the light wind. Someone must be inhabiting one of the cottages on either of the Wapomeo Islands. Vaguely she recalled hearing that a doctor might be renting the one on Little Wapomeo which was owned by Taylor Stratton. Doctor Howland, that was the name, not someone Harriet knew and hopefully not someone Father knew. Strange though, the voices sounded like two people arguing. The wind picked up a bit and rustled the leaves making it impossible to pick out individual words.

Harriet laughed under her breath. "Heavens, I'm getting as bad as Annie. Listening to things that have nothing to do with me." She turned to head back into the bush, having taken note of her position and intending to bear a bit further to the east when she came off the ridge. The voices rose above the wind again, still unintelligible. A muffled sound echoed across the water, like someone striking a melon with a wide stick and the voices cut off at the same time. "Now that's odd. Maybe the argument, if that is what it was, concerned who should be chopping wood for the fire." Shaking her head and pushing the incident from her mind, she walked a bit further along the top of the ridge. From the direction of the Blecher cabin came the mutter of their outboard motor, Harriet glimpsed the craft heading toward the twin islands with the younger Martin and his sister on board. A tarp covered a fairly large mound of something in the bow of the vessel. "Lord only knows what that's about," Harriet muttered. She half walked, half slide down the ridge and then up a small rise and there, nestled in the hollow was the place she sought. Taking some wool from her pocket, she tied some to branches as she made her way back toward the lodge. It was after one o'clock by the time she came out onto the trail near where she'd met Tom and Shan earlier.

"Hello Mark," Harriet greeted the tall, angular park ranger, popping out of the bush and startling him.

"My stars, Miss St. George. You did give me a start. No paintbox today?"

"Not this morning. I went in search of a certain hollow in the bush that I came upon by chance earlier in the year but hadn't been able to locate since."

"Have any luck today?"

"I did." She smiled brilliantly and then motioned him closer. "I have a secret to share with you."

"Nothing scandalous, I trust." Robinson seemed a bit uncomfortable.

"Nothing about my father, as I suspect you are already in possession of that information. No, this concerns you and the bet for the big trout."

"Oh?" Mark relaxed a little. "What have you heard? Did they manage to hook him this morning?"

"Not exactly." She smiled. "I met up with Tom and Shan first thing this morning coming back from Joe Lake. They didn't catch the big one, but Tom said he was going out for a day or two, up to Tea Lake I believe, and see if he could catch one nearly as big so he could pass it off as the one you men are seeking. He was very amused to think he was planning to put one over on you."

"The scoundrel!" Robinson mimed annoyance, but his eyes were full of mirth. "I wish I had thought of that," he confessed.

"I thought it only fair I warn you." Harriet grinned.

"I thank you for that, Miss St. George. And may I say I am sorry to hear about the trouble with your father."

"Don't bother your head about that, Mark. In many ways I am better off without the ties of family." She grimaced. "At least now, no one can marry me off to a man of their choosing. If I decide to marry it will be to someone of my choosing."

"I am happy to hear you're not overly upset over the situation then. Thank you again for the information, now I must be going. I have a lead on those bootleggers, someone let drop there is going to be a delivery today." The ranger touched his cap and stepped by her on the trail.

"Good luck, Mark. I hope you catch them red handed." Harriet waved and continued down the trail. She glanced at the sun which had decided to show its face, if the weather held there was time to fetch her paintbox and get a good hour's worth of painting down before the light failed beneath the canopy of leaves.

There was no sign of Shan or Tom when she arrived at Mowat Lodge. Tom's distinctively coloured canoe was missing, so he must have already left on his quest. She grinned. Turnabout was fair play in her book, tipping Mark off only added to the drama of the fish bet in her opinion. After checking on her canoe, she headed toward the lodge. Rounding a corner of the building she stopped short. Across the bare patch of land between the lodge and the outbuildings, Shannon Fraser, Belcher Sr., and the disreputable man she'd seen with Fraser much earlier in the season were engaged in a heated discussion.

Harriet set her gear down being as quiet as possible and slipped into the shadow of the lodge. She made her way toward the men, skirting the rear of the buildings, treading carefully through the weeds and long grass. Peering around the corner of the woodshed, she withdrew her head quickly. The men were only a few paces from her place of concealment.

"Delivery made?" She recognized Fraser's voice.

"*Ja*, Martin took it this afternoon." That was Belcher Sr.

"Alone? What if something went wrong?" Fraser again.

"*Nein*, Bessie went with him. Looks better for a woman to be along, more innocent like. A day of fishing by the dam." The man glanced over his shoulder. "I let her take the pistol hidden in her skirts. There was no trouble."

"Better not have been. Them men don't like it if the delivery is late." That was the third man. "That Frenchie gets mighty perticuler like if things don't go his way."

"No need to worry. The delivery is made. I saw the motor launch returning before I came to meet you." Blecher again.

"Fine and good. Let's drink to another successful run." Fraser rubbed his hands together and motioned toward the lodge.

"Not me," the third man shook his head. "I got places to be."

Harriet blinked in the dying light and to her surprise in that amount of time, the rough clad man faded into the gloom. Holding her breath, she slunk back toward where she left her gear. Reaching it without being discovered, she picked it up and went toward the lodge, crossing paths with Fraser and Blecher Sr. as she approached the steps. It seemed a better idea to hang around the lodge and see what she could hear rather than heading into the bush. Some of the locals had reported seeing a black bear with two cubs scrounging in the undergrowth not too far from where she planned to paint. There were plenty of dandelions growing in the clearings where the tree canopy was thin.

"Evening." She nodded at the two men and hurried by them. Her mind worked overtime as she mounted the stairs to her room. Bootlegging, it had to be bootlegging, and they must be selling the liquor to the aboriginal peoples living nearby. Tom, she knew, was opposed to the selling of liquor to them. Winnie had mentioned that he was planning to speak with Mark Robinson about his suspicions. In the act of kicking her door shut with her foot and dropping her gear on the bed, the image of the Blecher boat returning across the darkening water of Canoe Lake this evening came to mind. She'd only caught a quick glimpse through the trees, but the bow of the launch had been empty of whatever it carried on the outbound journey and no strings of fish were visible hanging over the side. At the time, Harriet had only noted it in passing, but now it started to make sense. She thought she'd seen something floating in the water by Little Wapomeo, just a dark shadow not far from the shore, but when she squinted her eyes hoping to improve her vision, the shadow seemed to be absent. A trick of the light, no doubt. She dismissed the memory.

"Blecher Jr. and his sister are deeply involved in the clandestine activities. I wonder if Tom has figured that out? I must ask Winnie when I see her tomorrow as I doubt Tom will be back tonight now that it's dark," she whispered. When faced with a problem it always helped Harriet to work it out by vocalizing her thoughts. Best to be quiet though. The Frasers, and especially Shan were formidable when crossed. Pushing the disturbing thoughts away, she completed her nightly ablutions and crawled into bed.

Chapter Nine

The morning of July 8, 1917, started like any other. Harriet was just finished up breakfast when a hue and cry went up out by the dock. She hurried toward the raised voices curious to see what the excitement was about. The Blechers were moored at the dock with a canoe tied to their boat. Breath caught in Harriet's throat as she got nearer, the distinctive gray-green colour of the canoe reflected in the still water. "That's Tom's canoe," she whispered. "But where is Tom?" She drew near enough to hear the discussion between the people gathered on the dock.

Shan was speaking. "I got him some provisions, and he left the dock about twenty-five minutes to one. He paddled down the lake and outside Little W, then he passed out of my sight between the two islands. Yeah, there were a bit of an east wind and some light drizzle, but nothing that should have caused Tom any trouble."

"My sister and I saw an overturned canoe floating about three-quarters of a mile from the Trainor's cottage. We just thought it was one of the Algonquin Hotel's that broke loose from Joe Lake portage. Colson keeps some canoes there sometimes. We didn't see any need to report it at the time," Martin Jr. said.

"What time was that?" Mark Robinson raised a suspicious eyebrow at the German American.

Blecher glanced at his sister. "Around about three in the afternoon, best as I remember."

"You didn't recognize the canoe as Tom's?" Robinson persisted.

Both Belchers shook their heads.

"Everyone around here recognizes Tom's canoe by that peculiar shade of green, and if it was bottom up, the colour should have been pretty visible," Harriet broke into the conversation.

Martin Jr. shrugged. "We just didn't pay any attention to it, and it was a quite a distance from where we were. Quite in the opposite direction we intended to be going."

Harriet kept silent, but her instincts were telling her the Blechers were lying, or at the very least hiding something. That, and the way they kept shooting glances at Fraser and their father, put her on alert. She was very fond of Tom and hoped that no harm had come to him. A jolt of realization shocked her. What was Winnie going to do if something had happened to Tom? Their engagement wasn't public knowledge yet, and if she was with child there were many who would be likely to believe the worst of

Winnie. Harriet glanced around, where was Winnie anyway? Someone needed to go and tell her. She left the men still hashing over the same details and set out along the trail toward the Trainor's cottage. Partway along she ran into Winnie who was rushing toward the lodge, her hair undone and flying behind her.

"What's happening at the docks? Father left without a word and paddled over leaving me to follow on foot." Winnie grabbed Harriet's arm and gasped for breath.

"Oh, Winnie. I don't know how to say this...it's about Tom—"

A smile brightened Winnie's face. "Oh, he must have caught that big fish he was after. Is he making the ranger make good on his bet?" She brushed past her friend and started forward.

"Winnie, wait. It's something else..."

"About Tom?"

Harriet nodded. "About Tom. They just towed his canoe in to the dock. Tom isn't with it."

"What are you talking about? How can he not be with it?"

"I don't know. Nobody seems to know. There's talk that maybe there's been an accident..."

"But that can't be true. Tom is a great swimmer and an experienced paddler, I mean he's a guide for heaven's sake. They must be mistaken."

"I saw the canoe. It's definitely Tom's."

"Who found it?" Winnie started to half run-half walk down the trail.

"I'm not sure who found it this morning, but the Blechers said they saw an overturned canoe floating by Little W Island yesterday around three. I think it was them who towed it in just now from what they were saying."

"Why didn't they say anything then? You said the canoe was just brought in this morning?" Winnie wiped tears from her cheeks but didn't slacken her pace.

"They *said* they thought it was one that broke loose from the Algonquin Hotel. I'm not sure I believe them."

"I don't like them. I've never trusted them. And that Martin Jr.," Winnie shuddered, "I just can't abide him near me. Always making sheep's eyes and trying to touch me." She stopped dead and regarded Harriet with wide eyes. "You don't think he did anything to Tom, do you? He might have found out about our engagement, I wouldn't put anything past the Frasers to have figured that out and anything they know, everyone soon knows."

"I don't know, Winnie. I really don't. But I promise you, we will find out what happened. Right now, we should get to the dock and see if they've organized a search party yet. No need to think the worst. Tom could have slipped getting out of the canoe and sprained his ankle or maybe broke something. He's probably sitting on one of those islands or along the shore somewhere waiting for someone to find him."

Winnie took a deep quavering breath and wiped her nose. "Yes, you're right. Of course, Tom is okay and has just hurt himself somehow. He's well able to spend a night rough, he's done it many times before." She gripped Harriet's hand. "C'mon, let's hurry. I want to be part of the search party. I'm sure between the two of us we'll find him. We know the bush almost as well as Tom does."

Nodding, Harriet hurried beside her friend toward the gathering by the lodge. *I hope I'm right and nothing horrible has happened. I don't like the way Frasers and the Blechers are behaving. What if Tom tried to do something about the bootleggers? What if one of them heard he was planning to tell the ranger what he knows, and who he suspects?* She reined in her rioting thoughts and forced herself to slow her breathing. *Don't go borrowing trouble. Tom is fine. I must hang onto that thought. Both for Tom and Winnie. Tom is fine. Tom is fine. We'll find him today. I know we will.*

The two women joined the cluster of people at the dock where Tom's canoe bobbed against the dock as if nothing was wrong and it was just waiting for him embark. Harriet turned her blurred vision from the sight. Beside her, Winnie gripped her hand so hard the knuckles hurt.

The discussion was still going strong. Mark Robinson was pressing people to form a search party and set out immediately to scour the shoreline of the lake and the two islands.

"Tom must be out there waiting for someone to realize he's in trouble and go looking for him. No time to waste, let's get moving," Robinson looked from one man to another.

"It don't look good. If the man was on shore somewhere surely he would have started a fire so the smoke would guide searchers to him." Shan shook his curly red-haired head.

"Tom's a good swimmer, so if he somehow ended up in the water, he would have swum to shore. Even if he was injured he would have made it to the shore," Robinson insisted. "I insist we form a search party immediately."

Fraser sighed and scratched his head. "George, Larry you want to join up with me and whoever wants to come along and search the lake and the shore?"

George Rowe and Larry Dickson went off to get some equipment, while Fraser stalked off toward the lodge, presumably to do the same.

"We can help," Martin Jr. offered. The three Blechers chugged off in the motor launch toward their cottage. Not doubt to inform Louisa Blecher that her husband and children would be joining the search for the missing man.

Hugh Trainor offered to search the shore and woods near his cottage and paddled off across the lake. Winnie trembled at Harriet's side, her gaze on the stretch of water visible between Big and Little Wapomeo. The narrow channel was choked with lumber which explained why Tom had skirted the other side of the smaller island when he set out. At least according to what Shannon Fraser said earlier.

"Winnie," Harriet tugged at her hand, "we can use my canoe to help search."

"Yes, yes. Let's do that. I can't bear just standing around waiting. Oh, dear God, I feel so useless. He must be okay, maybe just broke a leg or something so he can't hike back."

"That may be true. Let's search the islands first. It's near where they found the canoe and if Tom did somehow end up in the water surely he would swim to the nearest land." Harriet led the way to where her canoe lay beached.

"He might have slipped or fallen in the bush and shoved his canoe out into the lake hoping someone would see it and come looking for him," Winnie hypothesized, hope buoying her voice.

"That sounds like something he would think of. Tom's a smart man in the bush." Harriet shoved the canoe into deeper water and held it while Winnie settled herself in the bow. Pushing off with one foot, Harriet neatly stepped into the craft and took up her paddle.

"Did you notice that Tom's working paddle was missing from his canoe?" Winnie's voice floated back to Harriet.

"You're right, it wasn't there. And the other paddle was tied in as if he was planning to portage. I wonder what happened to the other paddle, and Tom's fishing rod and line was missing too. He always stowed it carefully so it wouldn't fall out in the event the canoe tipped in a storm or overturned. I wonder if the Blechers have it and just forgot to say so." Harriet matched her paddle strokes to Winnie's.

"That is strange. I didn't think to look for the rod. Oh, I do hope Tom is safe and sound and waiting for us on the island. Which do you think first?"

"Little W is nearest to where the canoe was floating, let's go there first."

"Tom! Tom! Are you near?" Winnie shouted when they were within hailing distance of Little Wapomeo. Her voice echoed across the water, muffled a little by the drizzle misting around the spruce trees.

The canoe bumped against the rocky shore. Winnie scrambled out and held the bow while Harriet joined her. They tied the painter rope to a convenient bush and set off to search the cottage and to circle the edges of the island. The cottage on the island belonged to a man named Taylor Stratton but Harriet knew the man wasn't in residence and the man renting it didn't seem to be about either. Nevertheless, the two women tried the door and found it unlocked. Shoving it open, Winnie hurried into the gloomy interior. Harriet followed, standing by the door. Nothing in the building was disturbed, there was no indication that anyone had been about.

"Oh, dear," Winnie leaned on the counter by the shuttered window, "I was so hoping that Tom would be here. It seemed the most likely place…"

"Come along, he still might well be sitting on a rock nearby waiting for us," Harriet encouraged her friend. In her own heart dread was forming. Commonsense told her that if Tom was nearby and at all conscious he would have heard them calling and sent some sort of signal. Maybe the other searchers were having better luck.

Winnie followed Harriet out of the building, pulling the door shut behind them. An hour's tramp of the shoreline and then quartering the inland parts yielded no better luck. Returning to the canoe, they paddled to Big Wapomeo. A few hours later, wet, tired and bug bitten, they gave up the exhaustive search of the island.

"He's just not here." Winnie dropped onto a large boulder and put her face in her hands.

Harriet rested a hand on the woman's shoulder, at a loss to find words to comfort her. Her own hope of finding Tom safe and sound were dwindling. There was no indication from the other searchers that they'd had any better luck. All the search parties, except the women's, carried shotguns which they would discharge if their search was successful. The sound carried well in the woods and would echo across the lake water, so far there had been nothing. Harriet narrowed her eyes through the misting rain and shook her head.

"Why would they go looking that far up the lake?" she wondered.

Winnie raised her head. "Who?"

"The Blechers. They're not looking around here at all but heading up the far end of the lake. I can't believe Tom would have gone that way or been that far from where the canoe was found. There was an east wind yesterday, I can't imagine how the canoe drifted to where they say they found it given the conditions on the lake."

"Who knows what they're thinking. I don't trust any of them as far as I could throw them. I can't believe they didn't recognize Tom's canoe earlier. I just don't believe them. And after that fight Tom had with Martin Jr... you don't think Tom's disappearance has anything to do with that do you?" Winnie glared down the lake.

"I couldn't say, Winnie. He does have a vile temper, and he's been known to be violent on occasion. Remember the time he swung that paddle at the tourist's head that bothered him out on the lake by asking questions? But for him to take on Tom...I don't know... unless he managed to take Tom unawares, I can't imagine Martin beating him in a fight."

Winnie straightened and got to her feet. "Yes, you're right, I'm sure. I'm just that worried I'm being paranoid. Let's get on with searching along the shoreline on the east side for a little ways. Then I suppose we can join the men looking in the bush."

"I think that's a good idea. We've done an excellent search of the islands and there's no way he's here, nor is there any sign that he has been here. So, he must be somewhere on the land." She gripped Winnie's hand. "We will find him. With all these people searching I'm sure someone will come across him or some sign of him before long."

Back on the water with the bow pointed toward the shore, the two women made quick time to a small marshy beach where they'd often landed with Tom. Pulling the canoe up the sand, Harriet tied the painter to a bush, making doubly sure the canoe would stay put. Shoving her hair off her face, she frowned across the lake, silently willing Tom to appear, or for the blast of a shotgun.

"I'm sure it was just an accident, but can you think of anyone else besides Martin Jr. who might wish Tom ill?" Harriet glanced at Winnie.

"I was just thinking the same thing. I don't know, maybe Shan? He still owes Tom that money for the canoes he bought in the spring. I know Tom asked him for it, but as far as I know he never received it."

"I heard Shan and Tom arguing about it the night of the Dominion Day celebrations," Harriet said.

"I think Shan and him had words about the bootlegging too," Winnie revealed.

Harriet veered away from the painful thoughts. "Let's not go borrowing trouble, as Great Aunt Lois would say. We're most likely just letting our imaginations run away with us. There's lots of places to look yet before we start to despair."

The women made their way along the shoreline for a distance of about a mile and then turned back. They searched further into the bush, watching for signs that anyone had travelled there. Spending time in the bush with Tom, who was a superb woodsman, taught Harriet the signs to watch for. They struck some deer trails and disturbed a beaver busy cutting trees for his dam, but no sign of Tom. The blast of a shotgun remained persistently absent. Dusk was falling and the insect swarms were increasing in their numbers by the time the women gave up their search.

The lake was still and smooth, broken only by the swish of the paddles and the hiss of water against the hull of the canoe when they made one last effort to search before the light faded completely. The sky was clearer, the first stars glimmering in the sky and reflected in the mirror surface of the water.

"I love this time of night, when the day is almost gone, and night is drawing in. But oh, my heart is sore with worry over Tom." Winnie tipped her head back to look at the sky. "I hope it doesn't rain tonight. I hate to think of him out there cold and wet."

"I have to admit, I'm worried too. I was sure someone would find him today, or at least come across some sign that he was about. It makes no sense. How could he just vanish into thin air?" Harriet said.

"And so close to where he started out. I just can't believe something terrible has happened to him...but Harriet, I'm so afraid that it has."

"If something terrible has happened, or someone has hurt Tom, I promise you we will find out what went on and who did it. Tom's my friend too and I won't rest until we unravel this mystery. If he's hurt, someone will pay. We just need to find him so he can tell us what happened."

It was dark when they reached the lodge. After stowing the canoe, Winnie agreed to stay at the lodge with Harriet rather than make the trek through the trail to her cottage. The men of the search teams were gathered in the dining room and looked up when the women entered the room.

"Just about gave you two up for lost," Shan greeted them, sucking a toothpick between his teeth.

"No luck with you either?" George Rowe asked.

Harriet shook her head. "We searched the islands and then the shore for about a mile on either side of where Tom likes to leave his canoe near there. No sign of him at all."

"Frist light, we'll head back out. There's a lot of bush to search, and if he's bad hurt he might not be able to call out. But we'll find him for sure tomorrow," Mark Robinson said. "I'm headed to my cabin, get some shut eye." He stood up to leave and was followed by Rowe and Dickson along with a fire ranger named McDonald who was familiar with Tom from the time they worked as fire rangers together.

Shan lurched to his feet and made to leave as well.

"I'm assuming the Blechers didn't have any luck either?" Harriet's question stopped him.

"Naw, they just putted around in that motor boat of theirs."

"I saw them headed up the lake toward Tea Lake Dam. Why in God's name would they go that far? What do they think they know that we don't?" Harriet watched his expression closely from behind veiled eyelashes.

Fraser's mouth twitched and a muscle ticked in his cheek, gone almost before she saw it. "Nothing as far as I know. Who knows what that family thinks anyway?" He moved toward the door.

"You seem awful friendly with them lately. I thought I overheard Bessie telling her mother about some *arrangement* her brother was making with you," Winnie chimed in.

"Wal, now where would you hear something like that?" Fraser swung around and stared at Winnie.

"I heard them talking. You know how sound travels across the water. They were just getting into their boat, and I was walking down to the shore in front of my cottage. I don't think they knew anyone was about. Martin was saying something about a meeting with you and some other man and that Bessie needed to stay clear of it." Winnie met his gaze. "You and them more involved in the bootlegging than you're letting on?"

Fraser took a step toward Winnie. Harriet picked up a heavy jug and held it by the side of her leg, just in case she might need to use it.

"If I am, and I'm not saying I am, it's none of your business. There's some things you best be forgetting about. Same thing I told Tom when he came nosing around asking the same kinda questions." He strode from the room.

Harriet replaced the jug on the table and let out a deep breath. "Are you sure that was wise? If Shan is involved with the bootlegging, and I know he is, challenging him about it might not be the best course of action. I need to tell you something, but not here. Come up to my room."

The two women crossed the hall and went up the stairs. Harriet unlocked her door and let Winnie enter first. Following her in, Harriet shut and locked the door. Tucking the key in her pocket, she offered Winnie the lone chair and perched on the edge of the bed.

"What is it? Does it have to do with Tom's disappearance?"

"It might. I'm not sure. It might mean nothing, and Tom will probably be found by tomorrow night. We just haven't looked in the right place yet."

"From your lips to God's ears," Winnie said. "But tell me what you suspect."

"The other night, two days ago I think. I was coming back from painting in the hollow I told you about and I'd just put up the canoe and was headed for the lodge. I came around the corner of the shed and there was Shan, Martin Sr. and that scruffy man who's always showing up at the oddest times."

"What's so odd about that?" Winnie frowned.

"There was just something about how they were huddled together in the shadows, like they didn't want to be seen. And they were arguing about something, it looked intense and not like a friendly meeting. So, I hugged the side of the lodge and went around the back way near the wood shed until I could hear then talking."

"About…"

"Shan was asking if the delivery was made, and Blecher said Martin Jr. took it that afternoon. Shan was worried about him going alone in case something went wrong. I set my gear down being as quiet as possible and slipped into the shadow of the lodge. Then I went toward the men, skirting the rear of the buildings, sneaking carefully through the weeds and long grass. Peering around the corner of the woodshed, I ducked back pretty quick. They were only a few paces from my hiding place. Then Blecher said that Bessie went with Martin Jr. because having a woman along made it look innocent." Harriet leaned over and lowered her voice. "He said he let Bessie take his pistol."

"Really?" Winnie gasped. "What on earth would they need a pistol for?"

"Then Blecher assured them there had been no trouble. The third man spoke for the first time and said there better not have been trouble because the men they were delivering to didn't take kindly if the deliver was late or confiscated. Blecher said it was done because he saw the boat coming back before he came to the meeting. The odd man said something about the Frenchie getting annoyed when things didn't go to plan. Shan said not to worry and suggested a drink to celebrate the successful run, Blecher agreed, the other man declined, and I swear he just vanished into the dark. It was creepy. Then I snuck back in the direction of the dock and made like I'd just got back."

"You think it might have something to do with the bootlegging? Tom is some upset about the trouble it's causing with some of the friends he goes trapping with from the Indian community."

"It might, most likely does. If Shan, or maybe the men who are taking possession of the delivery, found out Tom was planning to talk to Mark Robinson about his suspicions..."

"Or Martin Jr. He was after me again yesterday and I told him I wasn't interested. I was engaged to Tom."

"How did he react?"

"Not well, as you'd expect." Winnie raised her gaze to meet Harriet's. "You don't think someone has done Tom a hurt, do you? Like a warning to keep his mouth shut."

"Maybe. I don't know." Privately, Harriet wondered if maybe someone had quieted him in a more permanent way. But that was silly. Tom was tough, it would take an army to bring him down and that would have caused noise. From where the canoe was found, any altercation involving more than two or three men would have been heard by someone.

"Did you see the Blecher's boat the day Tom left the dock? I didn't notice anything." Winnie frowned.

"I did, now that I think about it. I was coming out on top of the ridge and happened to look down at the lake. Bessie was sitting in the front and Martin Jr. in the back, but in between them was a something big covered by a tarp. Maybe a wooden box or container of some sort."

"They must be in on the bootlegging. I bet that's what I heard Tom and Martin Jr. shouting about a week or so ago. When I asked Tom about it, he said it was nothing important and to forget about it. He didn't *look* like it wasn't important though."

"Stay here tonight, Winnie. I've got the chills just thinking about all this. You can have the bed. I'll sleep on the floor."

Winnie eyed the bed. "It's narrow but it should hold two if neither of us thrash about. It's not fair for you to have to sleep on the floor, and I don't want to either." She laughed.

Harriet giggled. "I'm game if you are. Just don't talk in your sleep."

Chapter Ten

The third day of the search went much like the ones preceding it. Winnie and Harriet met with George Rowe, Larry Dickson, Mark Robinson and of course Shannon Fraser.

"There's no way Tom is in the water," Mark insisted. "The man is too good a swimmer and a canoeist for him to have fallen out of his canoe. I say we should concentrate on combing the bush, if he was disoriented for some reason he may have wandered farther into the woods than we thought."

Rowe and Dickson agreed. Fraser pointed across the water where the Blecher's motor launch was putting along the shoreline far up the shore from where the canoe was found. "Looks like someone don't agree," he commented.

"They'd be a lot more help looking in the bush." Winnie shoved her hands on her hips and glared at the departing boat.

"At least they're helping," Harriet attempted to cool Winnie's temper.

"Are they?" She continued to glower down the lake.

"We're wasting time." Mark pulled out a rough map of the area and spread it out on a rock. "Here's where we looked already." He pointed to an area crosshatched with pencil marks. "George, you take this bit. Larry, you try here, and I'll go up this way a bit." The ranger pointed out the places on his map.

"What about us?" Harriet broke in.

Mark regarded her solemnly for moment and then flicked his gaze toward Winnie. "Why don't you two go over the shoreline again directly opposite where the canoe was found, and maybe up the lake a ways." He folded the map and indicated to Harriet he wanted to speak with her alone.

"Winnie, could you go and fetch some lunch for us from the lodge. I'm sure Annie can supply some bread and cheese." Harriet nodded at her friend.

With reluctant feet and a few backward glances Winnie hurried up the path to the lodge.

"What is it, Mark?" Harriet moved closer to the ranger.

"I'm beginning to worry that something bad has happened to Tom and if we do find him I'd rather the Trainor woman wasn't there. I still don't believe he's in the lake, but something is certainly wrong, or Tom would have found a way to send some sort of signal so we could locate him."

Harriet nodded. "I've had the same thought myself." She hesitated and caught her bottom lip between her teeth. "Do you think his disappearance might have something to do with the bootlegging operation that's going on around here?"

"Why would you think that?" Mark's reply was guarded, eyebrows raised in surprise.

"Just something Tom said in passing," Harriet hedged, unsure of how much to reveal. What if the ranger was part of the gang?

"What did he tell you?" Mark lowered his voice.

"Nothing much. Just he had some suspicions and was going to speak with you about them. Did Tom ever bring up his suspicions to you?" Harriet watched the man's expression carefully but saw only confusion.

"No, any time I've seen Tom lately Shan has been with him or within hearing distance. I don't imagine he would bring up anything sensitive unless he was sure of not being overheard." Robinson frowned. "I would dearly love to know what it was he thought he knew."

"I got the lunch," Winnie joined them, somewhat breathless from her hurry. "What are you talking about?" She glanced from Mark to Harriet.

"I was just showing Harriet where I thought you should search today." He indicated the area of the shoreline on his map.

"We've already looked there," she protested.

"Yes, but maybe one or the other of us have missed something, some small clue that might give us an idea of where else to look," Harriet said.

"I suppose that could be true. Women tend to pay more attention to little details than men do, if I do say so myself," Winnie agreed.

"I'll be on my way then." Mark folded his map and tucked it in a pocket. "If you find anything at all give a shout or hit the water with a paddle. The sound will carry far in the bush."

"We'll meet back here at sunset," Harriet said.

"We have to find him today. It's been too long. I'm really scared and starting to think Tom's never coming back." Winnie gasped and grabbed Harriet's hand. "You don't think he set this all up do you? Maybe he doesn't really want to marry me or take care of me and the baby. Maybe he just up and ran off..." Unshed tears shone in her eyes.

"Do you honestly think Tom would do that? It would be one thing if he just disappeared, but to leave his canoe floating like that. I can't imagine he would put his friends through all of this worry, and he would know we'd keep searching for him until we found something. Tom wouldn't do that to us," Harriet assured her.

"What if there's nothing to find?" Winnie's voice broke on her sobs.

"There is something and we will find it eventually," Harriet said fiercely. "I'm going to search now, standing here speculating isn't doing anyone any good. Are you coming?" She picked up the knapsack with the lunch and turned toward the trail that would take her to the area she wished to search.

After a pause Winnie followed her with much sniffing, coughing, and the occasional sob. The sun was high overhead, and the heat beat down even through the canopy of leaves overhead when Harriet called a stop for lunch.

"Here, you need to eat." She handed bread and cheese to Winnie.

"I'm not hungry. I can't eat or I'll just throw it up," Winnie protested.

"You need to eat, not just for you but for the baby," she insisted, pressing the food into her hand.

Winnie took the offering and nibbled on the cheese, a single tear tracking down her cheek.

Harriet repacked the knapsack with any refuse and led the way along the route she'd chosen. Her eyes scanned the bushes which crowded the shore and sometimes impeded their passage, alert for any sign of footprints, disturbed soil or indication that a person had passed this way recently. The biting insects swarmed when the undergrowth was disturbed which did nothing to improve her mood. *Honestly, if Winnie doesn't stop whinging soon I'll drown her myself.* Harriet tamped down the uncharitable thought and pushed on. The sun was dipping low through the trees across the lake and sending red-gold lights dancing on the waves that ruffled the lake when Harriet called a halt.

"I think this is the extent of the area Mark asked up to search." She tipped her head toward the angle of the sun. "If we want to make it back to the lodge before dark we need to turn around now. Otherwise, they'll be sending a search party out for us."

Winnie nodded without speaking, shoulders slumped in defeat. "We're never going to find him."

"Something has to turn up." She stopped speaking at the sound of a motor chugging down the lake. "Even if the worst happened and Tom ended up in the water like the Blechers seem to think," she held up a hand to stop Winnie's denial, "even if, the lake is shallow near the islands, only about thirty feet in depth and the water is warm this time of year." She swallowed hard before continuing. "Even if the worst has happened, the body would have come to the surface by now..."

"I suppose you're right, but I just can't think straight right now. I can't imagine never seeing him again...I just can't" Winnie set off at a quick pace and Harriet hurried to keep up with her.

The search parties were gathered on the landing when the two women emerged from the bush trail. Harriet caught Mark's eye and shook her head; he grimaced and shook his head as well. Winnie stopped before they reached the dock.

"I'm going home, back to the cottage. I need to be alone right now." With lowered head she hurried away from the group, tripping now and then on a loose stone or root.

Harriet joined the men and listened to them report on their search. The Blecher motor launch bumped into the dock where Bessie held it steady with her hand.

"Nothing," Martin Jr. reported. "We're headed home now for some supper."

Bessie shoved the boat away from the dock and Martin steered toward their cottage.

"Don't know why they insist on looking in the lake, not a chance Tom would end up drowned," Mark said watching the wake of the departing boat lap at the pilings.

"Until tomorrow then?" Harriet said, "Meet here as usual?"

Mark nodded and then gathering dispersed.

* * *

The eleventh of July was clear and hot. Harriet tramped through the bush solo, Winnie having cried off accompanying her on account of feeling ill. It was almost easier to be on her own with no constant complaints or whinging, although she could understand Winnie's unease. Seeking higher ground and hopefully a clearing where the sun could get through and discourage some of the flies, Harriet hiked up the ridge. Grasping the slender trunk of a sapling to aid her tired legs she hauled herself the last few feet and then turned to look down on the lake. She shaded her eyes when she caught the flash of sunlight on the wake of a boat and wished she'd thought to bring a spyglass with her. The boat moving across the water was the Blechers as no one else had a motor launch, the middle area was empty of cargo, but something was making a large wake behind the boat although they appeared to be travelling fairly slow. "What is that?" she muttered. Holding the tree for support she leaned forward as if that small amount of distance would make it clearer. "They're dragging something behind them, but what and why would they do that? It's not a log, it's not riding high enough in the water for that, and why would they drag a log anyway?" Harriet blinked and narrowed her eyes to cut the glare of the sunlight dancing on the waves. The boat disappeared between the two Wapomeo islands and was lost to her view. "Well, wasn't that strange?" she whispered. "I wonder what on earth they're up to now. It must be something to do with the bootlegging business. I must find an opportunity to speak with Mark about it."

The Blechers appeared on the other side of the islands, coming a bit closer to where she stood. There didn't appear to be anything behind the boat now and in her opinion the wake was much less than it was earlier. She shook her head; it must have just been a shadow on the water or a trick of the light bouncing off the wake of the boat. "Maybe you just don't like them or trust them and you're being paranoid," Harriet chided herself.

Finding a convenient rock in the sunlight she ate her lunch and then struck off to continue her search. She returned to the lodge with a heavy heart. The longer they went without finding any sign of the missing man, the more she was sure there was something terribly wrong. From the glum look of the other searchers, the feeling was mutual.

"Has anyone notified his family in Owen Sound?" Harriet asked.

"Sent a telegram to the family. I believe his brother may come out and join the search," Mark said.

"Never pleasant to get the news a family member is missing," Harriet commented. "I'm exhausted. A bit of supper and then I'm for my bed." She nodded in farewell to the men and took the path to the lodge.

* * *

The search continued with Harriet losing hope with each day that passed. Even Mark Robinson was less certain that Tom would be found alive and well. How long could an injured man survive in the rough without any aid? Harriet wondered. Tom hadn't started a fire, or the searchers would have seen it or at least smelled the smoke. Her gut clenched while she struggled not to accept what was becoming more apparently inevitable. Winnie had taken to her cottage the last few days refusing to see anyone, so Harriet visited her every evening to relay the failure of the searchers.

July 16th brought an end to the waiting and speculation. Harriet beached the canoe and took the path toward the lodge. Shouts of excitement echoed across the lake making her turn and shade her eyes.

"I wonder if that's good news or bad?" she muttered. "After all this time I can only imagine it can't be good, but maybe there will finally be some answers." Returning to her canoe, she shoved it into deeper water and paddled toward Little Wapomeo which was where the voices seemed to be emerging from. Ten minutes later she rounded the end of the island and let the canoe drift forward.

A man she didn't know was standing on a rocky point of the island shouting across to a canoe being paddled by George Rowe and Larry Dixson. Harriet dipped her paddle and then let the momentum carry her closer.

"To your left! Can you see it?" The man pointed to something in the lake.

Harriet craned her neck but could make out nothing in the dark water on the far side of the other canoe. She stroked the paddle through the water and moved closer to the man on the island.

"Son of a bitch," George Rowe's voice sounded choked and thin.

"Oh my God!" Dickson poked at something in the water.

"What is it?" The man on the island yelled across.

"It's a body. Looks like Tom's shirt," Rowe called.

"Oh my," Harriet gasped and covered her mouth with her hand. "Oh, no." She paddled to the edge of the island and stepped out of the canoe. "Hello. I'm a friend of Tom Thomson, I've been helping with the search since he disappeared." After securing the canoe, she offered the man her hand. "Harriet Agnes St. George.

"Dr. Goldwin Howland, Miss St. George. It's a pity to meet you under these unfortunate circumstances."

"Yes, this is most distressing." Her gaze was fixed on the two men in the canoe.

"Can you drag the body to the island?" Howland called.

"Working on it," Dickson grunted out the words.

With a minimum of splashing, soon the bow of the canoe faced toward Harriet and the two men bent to their paddles. Her stomach clenched at the sight of something bobbing behind them. *Oh, Tom. What happened to you? I'll never believe you just drowned by accident.* Another thought crossed her mind almost before she finished her first. *Or were you hurt before you ended up in the water?* Harriet shoved her hands in her pockets to hide the trembling. *Maybe it's not Tom. It could be someone else, lots of men wear plaid shirts.*

The canoe came alongside the shoreline and Rowe threw the end of a line to Dr. Howland. "I don't think you want to haul him out of the water just now, but tie that off so he don't go drifting off."

"Best thing to do is get Mark Robinson out here. He can make the official identification, and he'll know who to call," Dickson said, his face pale and set.

"Yes, yes. Of course. Get whoever you think is the right authority out here as soon as possible." Howland pulled the bloated form into somewhat shallower water and tied the line off to a sturdy pine tree. He turned to Harriet. "Are you quite all right, miss? I gather you were acquainted with Mr. Thomson."

"Yes. He is...was...a friend. We painted together. Oh, how awful for him to end this way."

"Should you return to the lodge now? It's not necessary for you to remain here." Howland gestured in the direction of the long, white two story building, out of sight behind the bulk of the island.

"No. I'll stay, at least until Mark gets here." She glanced at the pale figure moving slightly as the lake breathed against it. "It's just so hard to believe. Tom was a strong swimmer and an excellent man on the water and in the bush. I just can't imagine what could have happened."

"Can I offer you a cup of coffee? Or under the circumstances would you like something a bit stronger? I have the makings in the cottage."

"Coffee would be wonderful. I don't drink spirits." Harriet nodded and forced herself to look anywhere but at the body.

"Will you come up to the cottage?"

She hesitated before pushing her shoulders back and taking a deep breath. "I would prefer to stay here, if it's no trouble. I know it must seem silly to you, but I don't want to leave Tom alone."

"As you wish. If you're sure you'll be fine on your own for a few minutes, I will go up and bring the coffee back shortly."

"Yes, thank you. It is most kind of you. I can't tell you how much I appreciate your kindness." She glanced away across the lake. "I imagine Mark will come quickly once he hears the news."

"Let us hope so."

Dr. Howland took the path up to the cottage, leaving Harriet alone perched on a boulder by the water's edge.

"Oh, Tom. Whatever am I going to tell Winnie, how am I to tell her? What happened to you?" she whispered.

Dr. Howland returned with two tin cups of coffee in hand. He gave one to Harriet and stood sipping the other. Presently, the murmur of voices and splash of paddles alerted them to a party approaching the island. Howland went to the shore and waved when the canoe appeared around the island. George Rowe and Mark Robinson beached the canoe a distance from where the body was tethered. Robinson strode toward them.

"Park Ranger Mark Robinson," he offered his hand, "and who do I have the pleasure of addressing?"

"Doctor Goldwin Howland, we met briefly, I believe, when I arrived by train." He shook the proffered hand. "I'm renting the cottage from Taylor Stratton for the week."

Robinson nodded, then noticed Harriet standing behind the doctor. "Miss St. George. I'm surprised to see you here."

"I was out on the lake when I heard people shouting, so I paddled over...and well then...I just couldn't go away. Such a terrible ending."

Mark's gaze fell on the rope tied to the pine tree, his throat working as he swallowed. "George said he was sure they found Tom's body, but I suppose we need to make it official." He turned to the doctor. "How did you find the body?"

"In actual fact, I didn't find it per se. I was down by the lake watching two men going by in a canoe, when I noticed something bob up to the surface of the water. It looked odd and seemed too big to be a fish surfacing to feed. Wrong time of day for that as well. I called out to the men and asked them to go and investigate what it was. They called back it was a dead body, so I asked them if they could tow it to the island. One of the men said they thought it was the man who has been missing for over a week. They got a line on it...him...brought it here where I tied the line to that tree, then they went to get you." He raised both hands in a helpless gesture. "That's all I know."

"Where did the body surface? How far away from here?"

Howland squinted at the lake, then turned to Rowe. "You can most likely answer that question better than I."

Rowe stepped nearer the two men. "It was about the same distance from the shore as to the island. Lord God, it's only a short ways from where he set out last week. We should have found him long before this if he was in the lake the whole time." Rowe shook his head and looked anywhere but at the body.

"Well, I guess we should get this over with." Mark wiped his nose on the back of his hand. He moved toward the pine tree, followed by Dr. Howland.

Harriet hung back, clutching the now cold cup of coffee in nerveless fingers. George Rowe stood with her, reluctant to be in close proximity to the bloated corpse. Robinson and Howland gripped the line and hauled the corpse to the shallow water at the shore.

"Give us a hand, would you," Mark called to Rowe.

"Yeah, sure." Rowe went to join them in turning the body onto its back.

Harriet ventured nearer, one part of her not wanting to see the wreck of her friend and the other half needing to see in order to make sense of the reality. Tom was dead.

Dr. Howland, assisted by Mark Robinson and occasionally by Rowe, examined the body as best as he could under the circumstances. Harriet stood near memorizing every word.

Knee deep in water, Howland began his assessment. "Miss St. George, would you be so kind as to record my findings please. There is pencil and notebook on the table in the cottage."

"Yes, yes, of course." Harriet turned to go and collect the items.

"I'll go and get them for you," George Rowe offered, clearly anxious to put distance between himself and the noxious corpse.

"If you like." Harriet sat down on the nearby boulder and took a steadying breath. "Who else knows about this?" she asked Mark.

"I didn't speak to anyone, but Fraser may have overheard Rowe yelling for me." He shrugged.

"No one has told Winnie Trainor then?"

"Not that I know of, but if Fraser did hear something you can be sure the news will spread like wildfire."

"Here you go." George Rowe thrust a notebook and pencil into Harriet's hands, effectively ending the conversation with Mark. He then retreated a fair distance from the field of operation.

"Ready to begin?" Dr. Howland glanced over his shoulder at Harriet.

"As I'll ever be." She got to her feet and stood on the bit of coarse sand behind the doctor and Mark.

He cleared his throat and bent over the body. "July sixteenth in this year of our Lord nineteen-seventeen. Victim is identified as Tom Thomson by Park Ranger Mark Robinson. Body appears to have been in the water for a number of days. There is marked swelling about the head with a four inch long bruise over the left temple. No other bruising apparent on the body that I can ascertain. Decomposition and putrefaction has set in with blisters on the limbs visible. On examination, air was observed issuing from the lungs and blood was noted coming from left ear. There is a quantity of fishing line wrapped around the left ankle, the end broken off. No other fishing gear present. Victim's watch stopped at one-oh-five p.m." Howland straightened up wiping his hands on his pants. "That's all I can do under the circumstances."

"I have it all recorded." Harriet closed the notebook.

"What should we do with him?" Mark asked, looking down at his friend.

"There's nowhere to store him. The decomposition is fairly well advanced. I would suggest the body be buried with all possible haste." Dr. Howland stepped out of the water and took the notebook and pencil Harriet offered him.

Robinson frowned. "I don't rightly know if we should move him. I need to notify the family that he's been found and get instructions from them what they wish us to do with the body. For now, he stays where he is."

"Goerge, let's head back to the lodge so I can notify the Thomsons in Owen Sound." Mark got into the canoe followed by Rowe and the two men set off across the lake.

"I should go and inform Winnie," Harriet said. "Are you comfortable staying here to guard the body."

"Yes, yes. I'll be fine. It's not like he's going anywhere." Howland's face twisted in a grim semblance of a smile.

"One would hope not," Harriet rejoined him. "Then I'll go now and break the sad news to Winnie." She untied her canoe and paddled away from the gruesome item bobbing in the shallow water. As she paddled her fingers dipped into the lake water. *How could his body have stayed submerged in such warm water. I remember Mark telling someone the lake is shallow between the islands and the shore, only thirty feet deep, if I remember correctly. I suppose he would have sunk immediately after drowning, if he really did drown, but then the body would have bloated with gasses, like that cow that got caught in the pond at home, and it would have come to the surface long before today. Tom, what in heaven's name happened to you?*

The canoe bumped against the Trainor dock and Harriet made it fast to one of the cleats. "Winnie! Are you here?" She climbed out onto the dock. "Winnie!"

"Who is it? Oh, Harriet, it's you. Have you news? Is Tom back?" Winnie hurried from the cottage wiping her hands on an apron.

Harriet swallowed hard and blinked. "There is news." She took Winnie's hands when she joined her and led her off the dock. "George Rowe and Larry Dickson found Tom this morning—"

"Where is he? I have to go to him." Winnie pulled her hands loose, looking about with wild eyes.

"Wait, there's more. You need to listen to me."

"What then?" Winnie shoved her hands on her hips. "Hurry, Tom must be half starved, how badly is he hurt? I need to be there for him. Has anyone told his family?" The words poured out of her.

"Slow down. Slow down, take a breath. Listen to me. Here sit down a minute." She dragged the other woman to a nearby stump and pushed her down on it. "Let me finish. They found Tom in the lake near Little Wapomeo...Winnie he wasn't alive when they found him. I'm so sorry."

"What do you mean? You aren't saying Tom drowned are you? That's impossible, you know he's such a strong swimmer." Winnie surged to her feet. "Why are you lying to me, Harriet? If this is your idea of a joke it isn't funny."

"No, it's not a joke. I happened to be paddling by when they found Tom. There's a Doctor Howland renting the Stratton cottage, he's the one who saw something in the water and asked Rowe and Dickson to investigate."

Winnie collapsed back onto the stump, shock and disbelief rendering her almost expressionless. "Then what?"

"Are you sure you want to hear this?"

Winnie nodded. "I have to. It just doesn't seem real."

Harriet shrugged and swallowed, attempting to push the image of Tom's face from her mind. "The two of them towed Tom over to the island, then one of them went to get Mark Robinson as the local authority in the Park. Mark identified Tom and Doctor Howland made an initial examination. Mark has gone to the lodge to send a message to Tom's family in Owen Sound."

"Where's Tom then?" Winnie started to get to her feet, but her face paled alarmingly before she subsided back onto the stump.

"Still by the island. The doctor is guarding the body."

"How does he look? I need to see him. Can you take me there?"

"Honestly, Winnie. I don't think you want to see him the way he is. Better to wait until Mark gets instructions from the family and they get him out of the water."

"Oh my God, my God. What am I going to do?" Winnie dropped her face into her hands. "What about the baby?"

Harriet knelt beside her. "I don't know, my dear. But I'm sure you will figure it out in time. Perhaps you could go visit your relatives in the States until the child is born and then come back. With or without the child as you choose."

"That could work, but oh, I just can't think of that right now." She gripped Harriet's hands. "You're a good friend." Winnie scrambled to her feet and swayed so Harriet was forced to steady her.

"Why don't you go lie down? Is your father home or away?"

"I believe he's gone over to the lodge. Mother is still in Hunstville, I'm sure Father will let her know." Her voice was expressionless and blank.

"He'll have heard the news then. I'm sure he'll be back soon. Please do go and lie down."

"Yes, I believe I will." Harriet followed her to the cottage door. "They never approved of Tom, my parents. I imagine they'll be somewhat relieved he's gone..." Winnie's voice trailed off as she stepped inside.

"Dear God," Harriet muttered returning to her canoe and setting out for the lodge.

* * *

Chaos reigned when Harriet approached the lodge door. The Frasers were in Annie's tiny office engaged in what appeared to be a heated, anxious conversation with Martin Blecher Sr. The scene set off alarm bells in

Harriet's mind. Mark Robinson was trying to maintain some semblance of order but was not having much luck. A crowd of locals milled about; hushed voices occasionally punctuated by louder exclamations of disbelief. She saw Winnie's father in the group.

"Have the Thomsons been informed?" Harriet drew Mark aside.

He nodded.

"Did they give any instructions on what to do with Tom?" Harriet asked.

"Nothing that I've seen. I can wait until tomorrow morning but if we haven't heard anything concrete by then, well then, we'll have to make do the best we can."

"I can't imagine they won't respond swiftly." Harriet patted his arm and went in search of some coffee to calm her jangled nerves. Her steps slowed as she neared the huddle inside the office. The voices of the occupants were strained, and she caught Tom's name on Blecher Sr.'s tongue.

"He didn't have anything to do with it, I tell you," Blecher Sr. hissed.

"You better hope not," Annie hissed in return. "There'll be hell to pay if there's any evidence the death wasn't an accident."

"Tom just angered too many people, people with a lot to lose. The man should have kept his nose out of other peoples' business," Shan growled.

"Hush up. Someone might hear you and get the wrong idea," Annie whispered, but her harsh voice carried to where Harriet stood in the shadows.

"I admit Martin has a bit of a temper and Thomson's manner provokes him, but he'd never go hunt the man down and attack him," Blecher Sr. attempted to sound convinced, but Harriet heard the undertone of uncertainty in his voice.

"The last thing we need is anyone looking into our activities here. The operation is too successful. I have no intention of losing that income." Shan loomed over the American-German. "It was bad enough that U.S. War Department man coming up here earlier in the year. We almost missed making a delivery because of him."

"*Ja, Ja.* That was bad. But we managed and no one was the wiser."

Shannon glanced toward the door. "I need to go talk with Robinson. See what information I can squeeze out of him."

Harriet slipped out of the shadow and hurried up the stairs. Near the top, she gripped the handrail as a wave of dizziness washed over her. Closing her eyes, she took a deep breath and waited for it to pass. Harriet had never fainted, and she wasn't about to start now. Her gut told her there was more going on than was apparent. Even though Dr. Howland proclaimed that Tom died by misadventure—what a stupid word— why not just say accident—Harriet could not reconcile that with what she knew of Tom

Thomson. Suspicions stirred in her mind and couldn't be put to rest. *It's all linked to that bootlegging scheme. I know it. What did Tom find out that was important enough to kill him in order to be sure he remained silent on the matter?* The thought made her stomach roil. *The bruise on his temple...if Tom was already unconscious or not breathing when he went into the water, that would explain a lot of things... dead people don't bleed and there was no water in his lungs, so he couldn't have drowned. Father would be pleased to know I learned something from him.* An ironic grin twisted her mouth. Her gaze fell on the spare paddle leaning in the corner of her room...the edge of the paddle, if you hit someone with that narrow edge, it would leave a mark much like the one she'd seen on Tom's temple. *Oh dear God, I'm sure Tom was murdered. Maybe, or maybe not, on purpose.* Harriet moved to the window and gazed out toward the two islands across the lake painted with the reflection of the sky. "I promise you Tom, I'll find out what happened, and if someone did murder you I'll figure out who it was and make sure they pay." Her fingers whitened where they gripped the windowsill. "And I'm fairly sure I know where to start."

Chapter Eleven

Harriet came down to the front hall of the lodge early the next morning, Shan was in the tiny office bent over something on the desk. It was unusual for him to be there unless his wife was present. He glanced up at the sound of her boots on the floorboards, tucking something into his shirt pocket. There was an element of secrecy in the movement that stirred Harriet's already agitated suspicions.

"Morning, Shan."

"Mornin', Harriet" He moved out of the office.

As he passed her one hand patted his pocket in an unconscious manner. As if he was assuring himself whatever the missive was it was safe in its hiding place. Harriet narrowed her eyes at his broad back as he left the building.

"What was that all about? Instructions from Tom's family perhaps? He must be going to share the information with Mark." Still examining her slate of suspicions, Harriet filled a cup of coffee and sat near a window, elbows on the table, chin resting on her hands. Steam from the cup rose in tendrils in the cool morning air, tantalizing her nose with the scent. In spite of temptation, she left it untouched while her gaze followed the patterns of the twisting vapour. "So many twists and turns, so many possibilities, but where does the truth lie? And too many people who might have wished Tom harm. But if my suspicions pan out, I should soon have some concrete evidence to relay to Mark and the Thomson family," Harriet whispered the words.

Heavy footsteps interrupted her reverie. "You know what they say about people who talk to themselves." Annie Fraser tromped across to stand by Harriet's table.

"Umm, well, yes." Harriet sipped her coffee. "It helps me organize my thoughts to speak them out loud."

Annie leaned over with her calloused hands flat on the tabletop. "Organize all you wish, my dear. But keep your thoughts out of other people's business. You hear?"

"Whatever do you mean?" Harriet blinked in what she hoped was an innocent manner.

"Just mind what I said." The older woman straightened up to her full height and glared down at Harriet. "No good comes of rooting around in things that don't concern a person." Annie nodded once and then left the room.

Somewhat disturbed and more curious than ever, Harriet finished her coffee. Time to have a few words with Mark Robinson.

She hiked out to the ranger's cabin, but found Mark gone. Returning to the lodge, she couldn't resist the somewhat macbre urge to paddle out to the island and look at Tom's body. Even though her mind accepted the reality of his demise, her heart was having a harder time coming to terms with it. Giving into her heart, she took her canoe around the end of Little Wapomeo where she found Mark Robinson, Dr. Howland, and a man she didn't recognize bending over the body. The paddle splashed the water and Mark looked up.

"Harriet, Miss St. George...what are you doing here?"

"I wanted to be sure the body was okay." She shrugged helplessly. "It just doesn't seem real..."

"Miss St. George." Dr. Howland nodded at her.

The third man jerked upright and stared at her. "Miss St. George! You are the last person I expected to find here. Your...er...father has told everyone you went to Toronto and were marrying that Featherswallow fellow he was squiring about town a ways back."

"Oh, hello Roy." Now she saw the man's face, she recognized the embalmer from Sprucedale. "Yes, well Father must have thought he needed to save face after I refused to obey his commands." She lifted her chin and sniffed. "I have no wish to marry now or anytime in the near future. It would be best if you didn't mention to anyone in Sprucedale that you've seen me."

"As you wish. I have no desire to enrage your father." Dixon turned back to the job at hand.

"What's going on?" Harriet beached her canoe and turned to Mark. "What are you doing with Tom?"

The ranger shrugged. "There has been no instruction from the Thomson family, so I've asked Mister Dixon to remove Tom from the water. He will prepare the body as best as he can, given the amount of time the body has been in the water."

"Oh, I see. Then what is planned?" Harriet was uneasy about the lack of arrangements from the Thomsons. Earlier, Shan and Annie had their heads together over a telegram that arrived recently, but Harriet had no luck in discovering the contents.

"When Mister Dixon is ready we'll wait for the undertaker Shan has contacted to remove the body to Mowat. It's a Mister Flavelle from Kearney, he brought Dixon here with him as he isn't an embalmer himself, but just a furniture maker," Mark said.

"I suggest the body be buried as soon as possible as there is nowhere to keep him cool and the decomposition is very advanced." Mr. Dixon looked up from his work. "I believe Flavelle brought one with us on the train."

Mark nodded. "Shan has arranged for Mister Flavelle to come with a suitable coffin. But it may take a bit of time, from the train it is one and half mile journey from the station followed by another mile by canoe to reach us here."

"Where are you planning to lay Tom to rest?" Harriet fiddled with a loose thread on her shirt. Somehow, the whole situation felt wrong, out of step with how she felt things should be.

"I believe internment will be in the little cemetery at Mowat. Fraser has arranged for a grave to be dug," Mark informed her.

"Surely, the Thomson family would have sent their preferences for the funeral arrangements," Harriet protested. "Why is Shan taking charge of everything?"

Mark shrugged. "Seems odd, I agree. But to the best of my knowledge there hasn't been instructions received from the family. He's asked Martin Blecher Sr. to conduct the service."

Harriet snorted at that revelation but held her tongue. He was the last man she would have picked to say the last words over Tom.

* * *

Harriet waited while the embalmer did his work, then sat with Mark until Mr.

Flavelle arrived with the coffin and some local men to help with the awkward burden. The body was placed with some difficulty into the wooden box.

"Shouldn't it be lined with lead or copper?" Harriet whispered to Mark.

"That is usual, but I believe that time was of the essence what with the condition of the body, and I'm afraid a few corners may have been cut."

She shook her head. "I just can't imagine his family not providing a proper casket, and not wanting to bring him home to Leith or Owen Sound."

"I can only go off what Shannon Fraser has told me," Mark replied, although his expression suggested he had his suspicions about the veracity of the information.

"I suppose." Harriet floated her canoe into deeper water and settled into it for the paddle back to the lodge, following the canoes bearing her friend's body. The rough wooden coffin was secured length ways across the gunwales of two canoes, with two men in each vessel to paddle.

Once they reached the docks, many hands lifted the coffin onto dry land. Harriet glanced around expecting to find Winnie in the group gathered by the shore. The woman was nowhere in sight. Thinking that was quite odd, Harriet stored her canoe and joined the huddle of people around the coffin.

Six men shouldered the coffin and set out for the small burial ground near Mowat Lodge. Harriet fell into step with the Frasers and other local people who trailed behind the pall bearers. Winnie arrived breathless and joined the procession, her face fixed and grim, eyes glassy with unshed tears. Flies plagued the group as their passage disturbed the grasses underfoot and the bushes as they passed. Harriet slapped at the swarm of mosquitoes, brushing them off her sleeves. The trip to the cemetery seemed endless and yet when the men set down their burden by the grave, it felt no time had passed.

How can it be ending like this? It seems so sordid and ignoble for Tom to be treated so. Where is his family and a proper minister or priest? And Blecher Sr., of all people, to read the service. This is just wrong, so wrong. And yet, there is nothing I can do to make it more acceptable. Yes, Tom is in awful shape, but still, what is the hurry to have him buried and gone? Somehow I sense the Fraser's hand in this, and possible the Blecher's as well.

Harriet's thoughts were interrupted by the thump of the casket against the bottom of the deep grave. She swallowed and offered up a silent prayer for the repose of Tom's soul, wondering once again how Winnie was going to manage. Martin Blecher Sr. stepped forward and held what passed for the funerary rights using Robinson's small Anglican prayer book which he always carried with him. Blinking back tears she refused to shed in public, Harriet stood aside while the men filled in the hole, the sound of the clods of earth hitting the casket echoing in her chest. When it was done, she lingered until the others had left. She knelt by the freshly turned earth and placed a spray of wildflowers and fern leaves on the grave in front of the hastily constructed cross that tilted drunkenly at the head of the mound. Inside the fenced-in area nearby, two markers stood alone. James Watson, a mill worker who died in an accident in 1897 and Alexander Hayhurst, eight years old, the victim of black throat diphtheria in 1915. She rather thought that Tom wouldn't mind their company over the eons.

"Rest in Peace my friend." She laid a hand on the grave, letting her tears fall now that she was alone. After a time, she got to her feet and retraced her steps back to the lodge. On the way she detoured to the Trainor cottage hoping to find Winnie, but seeing the cottage was deserted, she continued on to the lodge.

She halted in the doorway of the entrance hall. Winnie Trainor was shouting at Shan about the shabby funeral arrangements. Not wanting anymore drama, Harriet avoided notice and hurried up the steps to her room.

Coming down much later, she discovered Mr. Flavelle and Mr. Dixon had left to catch the train back to civilization. Winnie was still pacing in the front hall, muttering to herself.

"Harriet! There you are." Winnie strode across to pull Harriet out of earshot of the office where Annie was sitting. "I can't tell you how upset I am."

"What's happened now? Where did you go after buried Tom? I expected you to be there for a while at least. I found I just couldn't leave him there alone when everyone left." Harriet pried the other woman's fingers off her arm.

"I need to contact Tom's brother, George. I have to go and find a phone and let him know what has gone on here. The Thomsons won't be happy, I can tell you. I need to set this right, for Tom. Help them in any way I can to get Tom back to them."

"His brother? But Shan said no one had heard from the family—"

"Shan is a liar," Winnie growled, "Thomson's sent a telegram informing Fraser they wanted Tom's body sent home to be buried in the family plot in Leith."

"A telegram? When did they send that?" Harriet swallowed hard. Her gaze darted toward the two Frasers huddled in the tiny office, her earlier suspicions given new life.

"Right after they found Tom, and Mark let George Thomson know." Winnie glared across the lobby.

"But what on earth would he have to gain by hiding that information?" Harriet's suspicions grew stronger.

"I don't know for sure, but I have my suspicions why they wouldn't want someone they didn't arrange for to look at poor Tom's body. I'm positive they have something to hide, something they don't want anyone to know."

"I'm afraid I have to agree with you on that score," Harriet said. "Oh, I wonder who this is?" A tall man stood in the doorway of the lodge, obviously looking for someone in particular.

"Excuse me, could someone direct me to where I might examine the body of Tom Thomson?" He spoke to the room at large.

Harriet exchanged a horrified glance with Winnie.

"Who might you be?" Shan strode across the room to confront the man.

"Why, I'm Doctor Ranney. The coroner from North Bay sent by the Thomson family to examine the body prior to transferring the body to Leith for burial in the family plot."

"There might be a small problem with that." Fraser hooked his thumbs into his belt and glowered.

"What could possibly be the problem? I was assured I would find the body at this location." Ranney frowned.

"The problem is Tom is already buried. We buried him this morning in the Mowat cemetery. You surely understand that after eight days in the water the body wasn't in any condition to leave lying about. The undertaker and embalmer recommended we take care of the burial as soon as possible. Which we did."

"Mister Churchill has been already? I understood he was coming later today?"

"Churchill? I don't know no Churchill," Fraser replied.

"Mister Churchill is the Thomson family's undertaker who is arriving with a coffin in order to transfer the body. Who are you referring to when you say undertaker and embalmer? I'm sure the family did not authorize anyone else." Ranney was firm in his speech.

"Well, you have to understand, we didn't hear from the family and things had to be taken in hand. So, I got the furniture maker from Kearney, Mister Flavelle to bring out a coffin and he, not being an undertaker or embalmer, brought Mister Roy Dixon from Sprucedale to prepare the body. We had a right nice little service for Tom, and he's buried in the little cemetery overlooking Canoe Lake." Fraser waved in the general direction of the burial.

"This is most unusual, I must say. I have no intention of digging up the body in order to examine it. Was there any examination done prior to the burial?"

"Why sure. Tom come ashore on the island where Doctor Howland from Toronto was staying, so he did an exam and the park ranger Mark Robinson watched him. He can tell you that I'm saying the truth about this." Fraser wiped the back of his hand over his mouth.

"I will need to see this Doctor Howland and any notes that were made. Can you arrange this?" Dr. Ranney looked somewhat dismayed and more than a bit annoyed.

"I can do that right away. We can use the Blecher's cottage, he's the man who spoke at the funeral. It was his son and daughter what found Tom's canoe floating between the two islands," Fraser assured him.

"If you would be so kind as to conduct me to this cottage and arranged for any people who might have useful information about the incident to be present also. Be sure Doctor Howland and the ranger are present."

Fraser nodded and led the coroner out the door. Winne and Harriet trailed behind them.

"This should prove interesting," Harriet whispered to Winnie.

"I wonder how many lies he and Blechers are going to have to tell to make sure they come off looking like heroes rather than the villains I'm sure they are," Winnie hissed back.

In due course Dr. Churchill arrived at the Blecher cottage, accompanied by

Shannon Fraser. There they were greeted by Martin Blecher, both Jr. and Sr. along with Bessie Blecher, Hugh Trainor and his daughter, Winnie, Geroge Rowe and Mark Robinson.

Blecher Sr. served beer and offered around cigars which seemed a trifle celebratory in a gathering to discuss the death of a friend. At least that's how it seemed to Harriet who lurked outside the cottage under an open window.

Dr. Ranney confirmed the date of discovery of the body, refusing the offer of spirits. "Could I see the results of your examination please, Doctor Howland?"

"Yes, of course." There was a rustle of paper being passed across the table. "Mark was kind enough to record my findings as I was knee deep in water at the time, as you understand. It was not conducted under the most ideal conditions." He omitted any mention of Harriet's presence at the exam, which was fine with her. Best to keep a low profile given her suspicions.

Ranney cleared his throat. "Yes, yes. Most unfortunate circumstances."

Paper scraped against the table; Harriet risked a quick look over the windowsill. The coroner had his head bent as he scanned the pages, flipping them over as he finished.

"Most unusual. You noted blood coming from the left ear. That could only occur while he was still alive. Corpses do not bleed, nor do they bruise. So, the contusion on the left temple must also have occurred while he was still living. And no water in the lungs...well I suppose that might be possible..."

Harriet caught her lip between her teeth, now more certain than ever that someone had done harm to Tom. *Perhaps with the intent to keep him quiet about what he suspected. Maybe it was only supposed to be a warning, but something went horribly wrong.* She ducked down below the sill again when Ranney raised his head to stare out the window.

"Tom, he might have stood up to have a piss over the side and lost his balance, hit his head on the gunwale or a rock when he fell," Fraser offered an explanation.

Harriet muffled a snort of disbelief and peered over the windowsill again.

"The man was too good a woodsman and canoeist to do that," Robinson objected. "It is far more likely, that if his death was due to a fall, he slipped while getting out of the canoe in water shallow enough that he could have hit his head on a rock when he fell."

"I suppose that is possible. Without actually examining the body, I could not say," Ranney sounded troubled. He flipped the notebook closed, tapping a few pages back into the dog-eared cover and handed it to Howland. He asked a few more questions and listened again to George Rowe describe how he and Larry Dixon came across the body. Mark Robinson insisted he felt there was no way Tom could have drowned in a lake he knew so well.

"And there is the issue of there being no water in the lungs. Surely if the man died by drowning there would be a fair amount of water in his lungs," Mark insisted.

"The body was very bloated and full of gases," Howland broke in.

"Again, without examining the body myself, I cannot comment." Ranney met the gaze of each person in the room. "Based on the evidence I have to hand I have to rule that Tom Thomson died from misadventure. In short, it was an accidental death."

Harriet ducked below the sill as the occupants of the cottage made ready to depart. In her gut she couldn't shake the belief that Tom was murdered. And what of the fishing line around his ankle. The suggestion that he sprained his ankle and tried to support it by wrapping fishing line around it was absurd. To begin with, if he had hurt himself that close to the lodge, surely he would have just paddled back to the lodge or halloed for someone to come and help. Sound travelled far and easily across water; everyone knew that. No, there were just too many unanswered questions and far too many suspicions.

She worked her way through the bush and arrived back at the lodge before the group containing Dr. Ranney, Shan and Winnie came trooping through the door.

Winnie drew her aside. "What do you think?" she hissed. "I saw you peeking in the window, so I know you heard what was said. Do you believe it was an accident?"

"I can't come to terms with that." Harriet shook her head. "It makes no sense. If Tom hit his head when he fell it might account for the blood and the bruise, but to drown he would have still had to be breathing when he went in. There would be water in his lungs. Therefore, I believe he must have already been gone before he went into the water. My question is, who hit him and who put him in the water? Was it just one person or more than that? And why for God's sake?"

"I think we know the why," Winnie said. "He was opposed to the bootlegging to the natives and was somewhat vocal in his intention to report his suspicions to the park rangers. Or it might have been more personal, maybe a warning for him to stay away from me? I know him and Martin Jr. have had words over me in the past."

Harriet glanced across the hall to where the Frasers and Blecher Jr. were speaking in low voices. Dr. Ranney waited, tapping his foot with impatience, for Shan to return him to the Canoe Lake train station so he could catch the next train to North Bay. It was a long journey, and it was obvious he was anxious to be gone.

"I'm taking the evening train to Scotia Junction," Winnie said. "I need to call the Thomsons and let them know what's happened and that Shan ordered Tom buried already instead of doing what the family asked. I'm sure his brother George will be angry as the whole family wants Tom returned home. I feel it is the least I can do for Tom. God, I can't believe he's gone. It's just so unreal." She wiped moisture from her cheek with the back of her hand.

"Are you travelling alone? Please be careful if you are. I agree Tom's family must be made aware of what has transpired. Although Tom might be happy to spend eternity in a place he loved so much, I'm sure his family would want him closer to them where they can tend to his grave." Harriet's throat closed on the last words.

"I'm travelling with another guest, Miss Terry. At least as far as Scotia." Winnie assured her. "I need to go. I can catch a ride to the station with Doctor Ranney."

"Yes, you go take care of things. I'm going to poke around here and see what I can turn up." She patted her friend on the arm and turned toward the stairs, then stopped. "Have you seen that odd little man around lately?"

"What man?" Winnie frowned and picked up her valise.

"You know, the one Shan was meeting with and the same man I saw with him and Bleacher Junior. I fairly certain he's their contact with the bootleggers."

"Not recently. But maybe a week or ten days ago, I did see someone who might have been the same man leaving the Blecher's late at night. I wouldn't have noticed except it was a bright night and he must have tripped on the path because he cursed load enough for me to hear him. I was on my way back from the privy."

"What can you remember? Do you think he was one of the natives? I've never been able to get a decent look at him."

"He sounded French, but he could be Metis I guess as easily as someone from Quebec. I have to go, Harriet. Miss Terry is waiting. Please be careful." Winnie hurried across the wooden floor, long skirts brushing the sand from the boards as she went.

* * *

Harriet struggled out of the twisted blankets which bore mute testament to her troubled sleep. Morning sun slanted through the open curtains of the second story room, highlighting bits of detritus left from her boots and trouser hems. She blinked bleary eyes and vowed to take Annie to task about the quality of her housekeeping, or lack thereof. On second thought, she might be better to let things lie. The last thing she needed was Annie snooping through her things and who knew what might *accidentally* disappear to be blamed on some passing crow who flew in her window, left negligently open by herself, and made off with something shiny. She dressed and gathered up her paintbox. There was no real urgency or, in truth, any inclination to put brush to board. But for appearances sake, she took them down to breakfast. Her real intent this morning was to make some sense of the knot of unanswered questions and suspicions churning in her mind. The door to the office was ajar when she passed. A quick detour showed her the place was empty with papers strewn haphazardly across the writing surface. Undecided, she hovered by the door. *If I could just look through those papers and maybe rummage through the drawers a bit. I bet I would find some interesting things about their operations. I wonder if I dare...*

"Something I can help you with?" Annie's voice was cold.

"Oh, you startled me!" Harriet took a step back from the office.

"Looking for something?" Annie's eyes narrowed.

"Umm, yes. I was looking for you. I wonder if I could use your broom for maybe a quarter of an hour this morning. I've made quite a mess of my room traipsing dirt in from my rambles in the bush." Harriet prevaricated.

"You have a problem with my housekeeping?" Annie took an aggressive step nearer.

"Of course not! I just don't feel it's fair for anyone to have to clean up such a mess."

"There's one in the cupboard under the stairs. Put it back when you're done." After a moment's hesitation and another glowering look, Annie pushed open the door of the office and shut it firmly behind her.

"Now I suppose I will have to go sweep my room." Harriet sighed and went to fetch the broom.

Twenty minutes later she returned the broom to the closet and forgoing breakfast, Harriet strode off into the bush along the trail she normally chose. Once out of sight of the lodge, she changed direction and circled back toward the Blecher boathouse. To the best of her knowledge, the Blechers were occupied elsewhere this morning, so it was as good a time as any to have a bit of search and see if it confirmed or contradicted her suspicions. *Perhaps I'll get lucky and discover what it is they hide under the tarp on their trips up to Tea Lake Dam.*

After making sure the cottage was indeed empty and that Louisa Blecher hadn't stayed behind when the rest of the family went off, Harriet wriggled through the thick bushes down the slight incline to the back of the boathouse. The door was unlocked, the padlock hanging by the shackle through the hasp. She winced at the squeak of the door as she pushed it open. The interior was dim after the sunlight outside. Leaving the door a little open, she moved down the boarded walk that ran beside the motor launch. A piece of canvas hung over the opening to the lake, letting in a bit of light now her eyes had grown accustomed to the gloom. The back of the boathouse housed a workbench with an array of tools that Blecher Jr. stored there.

To her dismay, the centre of the launch was barren. There were marks on the bottom boards where something heavy had rested, but no indication of what that might have been. A folded canvas lay under the deck of the bow. *Dare I get in the boat and see what if anything is under there? If someone comes along I'll have nowhere to hide...but I wonder....* Before commonsense could prevail, Harriet stepped into the boat, glad she'd left her paintbox secreted some way back in the bush. The vessel rocked against the walkway as she entered so she steadied herself with a hand on the gunwale. Making her way to the bow as carefully as possible she knelt and pulled the folded canvas toward her. The scent of raw mash whisky rose from the material and threatened to make her sneeze. Pinching her nostrils together with one hand, she pulled the canvas further out and ducked her head to look into the apex of the bow. Something was wedged against the side of the boat; laying on its narrow edge was a paddle. Harriet reached under and slid it toward her. *A canoe paddle! Not one a person would normally use for a boat like this one. Tom's favourite paddle was missing when the canoe was found. Is this his? Maybe it's just innocent. Blechers found the canoe, perhaps they just stowed the floating paddle and in all the chaos forgot to turn it over...but why then hide it under the bow of their boat? Why hide it all? I've come looking for answers and found only more questions...*

"Why is the boathouse door open?" Martin Jr.'s voice came clearly through the silence.

"You must not have locked it," Bessie accused her brother. The voices came nearer.

In a panic, Harriet shoved the paddle back where she found it and replaced the folded canvas as best she could. Where to hide? There wasn't room under the bow to go unnoticed in the daylight. Nor was there time to climb up into the rafters and hope no one looked up. Taking a deep breath, she threw her leg over the side and slipped into the water, cursing the wavelets that rocked the boat and lapped at the side of the boathouse.

"Who's there?" Martin Jr.'s voice was heavy with menace.

"Don't be silly, no one's there. You're just being paranoid. Why would anyone be in our boathouse?" Bessie chided him. *Mutter* makes sure no one trespasses." She giggled. "Remember when she chased that park ranger off with a broom? And all because he thought our stars and stripes shouldn't fly above their red ensign. Such nonsense."

"You never know. Lot of people been asking questions about the death. We never should have said we found the canoe. I told you so." Martin Jr. was out of breath. "Should have left it float there. Better if the body had never some to the surface too."

The door to the boathouse swung open and light flooded in. Harriet kept her head above water and peered out from under the walkway where she'd hidden herself. *Well, this might prove interesting after all. What did Martin mean, they never should have said they found the canoe. Did they know where it was the whole time Tom was missing?*

"See, I told you no one was here," Bessie crowed in triumph.

"I'm not so sure. Look at the canvas, it's been moved. I'm sure of it." The boat tilted when he got in, creating small waves that forced Harriet to hold her breath until they quieted. "Someone's been in here. The canvas isn't where I left it and" his voice became muffled as if he had stuck his head under the bow, "and the damned paddle is moved too."

"I'm sure it's nothing, *bruder*. There was much wind last evening, the boat must have moved about a bit and shifted everything. You worry too much. *Vater* says all is fine and the deliveries can continue as planned for the rest of the summer. Come, I'm hungry and *Mutter* is preparing sauerbraten for lunch."

The boat lurched and Harriet held her breath while the water lapped over her face. "You must be right. Nothing is missing and only a bit out of place. We must get rid of the paddle though. I don't know why we didn't leave it with the canoe. It was stupid to keep it."

"You know why we kept it. The edge of it was bloody and *Vater* wasn't sure the lake would wash it all off. I tried, as you know, but the stain refused to disappear."

Footsteps echoed on the walkway, then the door snicked shut followed by the click of the padlock shackle sliding home. Harriet took a deep breath and swam to the open end of the boathouse, glad she was wear trousers. More than anything she wanted to collect the paddle and take it directly to Mark Robinson. He would believe her, even if no one else would. But the Blechers, especially Martin Jr., were worried about the paddle. Moreso now that he thought it was moved from its hiding place. Which it had been, she supposed. But how to go forward? Abandoning the idea of securing the paddle for the moment, she ducked under the canvas covering the large boathouse door and swam around the side of the structure away from the cottage. Making as little noise as possible, she waded out of the lake and dodged into the bushes on the shore. Retrieving the paintbox required some backtracking, her soaked clothing clung to her body hindering her progress. With a sigh of relief, she collected the box and set off back toward the lodge. The heat of her body and the sun dried her shirt in no time, but the waist and hems of her trousers remained quite soggy.

"What in the world have you been up to?" Annie demanded.

Harriet paused on the doorstep. "I got overheated hiking and then missed my step when I was filling my canteen." She shrugged with what she hoped was a wry grin, even though her heart was pounding. "Ended up in the water." *There's no way Annie could know where I was. It isn't possible. Calm down.*

"Seems to be a lot of that going around. You should be more careful." Annie skewered her with a pointed look.

"Yes, well. I believe I will go and change into something a bit drier." Harriet moved toward the stairs.

Annie sniffed hard through her nose and retreated into her office.

Once in her room, Harriet set the paintbox down and stripped off the wet, grimy clothes. Pulling on a flannel shirt and dry trousers she sat down hard on the edge of the bed. Her fingers itched where she'd touched the paddle. *Bessie said the edge was bloody, does that mean what I think it does? Tom's blood, from where he was struck in the head? But who hit Tom? Not Bessie, I'm sure. But Martin Jr. has a wicked temper, and he was at odds with Tom over Winnie, not to mention the bootleg aspect. Perhaps he sought to solve two problems with one stone, so to speak? I'm not sure that makes sense, though. Why kill Tom? Shan has that look on his face the last few days, as if he knows more than he lets on. Does that explain why he ignored the telegram from the family and had Tom buried so quickly before the official coroner could get here? And what of the telegram the coroner said he sent informing of his arrival. The telegram Shan said they never received. More questions and no answers. Oh, my head hurts.*

Harriet collapsed back on the bed, bare feet hanging over the edge. Nothing was making sense, but some of it was starting to make far too much sense. There were missing pieces to the puzzle, but one thing was clear to her. Somehow, the Blechers and the Frasers were involved and that odd man with the French accent...how did he fit in? Finally, the exertions of the morning caught up with Harriet and she let her eyes close.

Chapter Twelve

It was dusk when her complaining stomach woke Harriet. Surprised at the lateness of the hour, she rose, straightened her clothes and pulled on socks and her moccasins. Padding down the stairs in search of food, she found Shan and a well-dressed man in the hall by the door.

She nodded hello and headed for the dining room, hoping there was something edible on the sideboard.

"I'm off now, Annie. This here is Mister Churchill, the Thomson's undertaker, come to take Tom home to Leith."

Shannon's voice caused Harriet to pause and listen, one hand on the doorpost of the dining room.

"At this hour?" Annie was plainly not in favour of the endeavour. "You can't be bent on digging up poor Tom at this hour of the night?"

"I have my instructions from the Thomson family, they are explicit. I am to exhume the body and transport it to the station to meet the first train to Owen Sound in the morning," Mr. Churchill informed her.

"You can't be expecting my husband to go out in the dark and help you dig up a corpse," Annie challenged the man, hands on her sturdy hips.

"Calm down, woman. I'm just taking the good doctor out to where we buried Tom and then coming right back. When the man is done what needs doing he'll send me a signal and I'll go back and fetch him and the coffin. Brand new coffin, too. Nice one. Musta cost a pretty penny."

"Since Mister Flavelle is a furniture maker and not an undertaker, I can only imagine that what he provided will be less than suitable. The family insisted on a proper coffin." Churchill cleared his throat. "If we might proceed..."

"Yup, the sooner we start, the sooner I can be back. Leastways the bugs won't be so bad at night as they would be earlier in the day." Shan rubbed his hands together. "I've got the coffin loaded on the wagon."

"Yes, let's be off. I have some lanterns to light the way and provide illumination while I work," the undertaker said. "The sooner I get back to civilization the better, and the family is anxious to receive their lost kin home."

Harriet hung back while the two men left the lodge. She was sorely tempted to follow them, but logistics held her back. It wouldn't be easy to go undetected and the thought of hiking through the bush in the dark wasn't appealing on any level. A bear and her cubs were sighted a few days ago, and she'd heard wolves serenading the moon last night. *No, better to wait here and see what I can glean from any conversation Annie might have.*

Under the pretense of getting some coffee, Harriet wandered into the dining room where she poured some thick dark sludge into a cup. With no intentions of drinking the stuff, she went out to perch on the edge of the top step leading down to the yard looking out across the chip yard. The position offered a decent view of the office if she turned sideways and leaned on the railing. The soft light of advanced twilight was gone from the sky, brilliant points of light glittered in the sable heavens. The lake was so calm the stars were mirrored on the smooth surface. Harriet breathed deep, there was no place on earth quite like the New Ontario bush wrapped in the arms of a summer night. She glanced toward the spot Shan would appear on his way back from dropping the undertaker off at the cemetery. It was a pity, she mused, that they'd buried Tom outside the ramshackle fence that delineated the boundaries of the burial ground. To the best of her knowledge, there were only two gravestones in the tiny enclosure. Although, with that big birch tree taking up a lot of the space inside the fence it might have been a problem to dig deep enough with all the roots that were surely planted deep in the sandy soil. Perhaps that was why they chose to bury Tom by the big spruce tree outside the enclosure. The way things were shaping up, it appeared the location of the grave was a moot point.

The light in the lodge dimmed as Annie snuffed out most of the lanterns. The woman glanced toward the open door and then disappeared in the direction of the Frasers' personal rooms. Harriet set her cup down and got to her feet, teeth caught in her bottom lip. *Dare I sneak a look at the office? Annie forgot to lock the door and Shan should be a while yet...I hope.* Toeing off her moccasins, she padded across the floor in her thick socks and lifted the latch on the office door. Little light seeped into the room from the hall, but it was enough to make out a pile of papers stacked haphazardly to one corner of the desk. Careful to make as little noise as possible, Harriet sifted through the sheets, some obviously torn from books, others just bits of scrap paper. The top ones were just an accounting of the room rentals and upcoming reservations for the rest of the season. Frustrated, she perched on the edge of the chair. Something rustled under the cushion when she put her weight on it. Intrigued, Harriet stood up and felt under the thin cushion. A sheaf of better quality paper came out in her hand. Moving closer to the door in order to make the best use of the dim light, she scanned the documents.

"Yes!" she whispered. In her hand were invoices of a sort, an accounting of the number of jugs of whisky, small barrels of beer and bottles of gin. Looking through to the bottom of the pile, Harriet took the oldest sheet and tucked it in her pocket. *With any luck it's old enough that they won't notice it's missing. I need something to take to Mark to prove what I'm saying.*

Feet crunched on the gravel footpath that ran along the side of the lodge. Her heart thumping double time; Harriet shoved the papers back under the cushion and tried to arrange the papers on the top of the desk in the same disorder she found them in. Fearing to waste any more time, she slipped out of the office and was standing on the bottom step of the steps leading up to her room when Shan appeared in the lodge door.

"What're you doing?" Shannon stomped across the room.

"Just came down to see if there was any coffee left." Harriet lied, crossing her fingers that the man hadn't noticed the cup she'd left on the front steps.

He grunted and hitched up his trousers. "Annie," he shouted. "Where in the hell is that woman?" he muttered under his breath.

Harriet moved toward the front door. *I left my moccasins out there and the damned coffee cup. That would be hard to explain if someone discovers them.*

"Where are you going?" Annie joined her husband, both now standing by the office door, frowning at Harriet.

"Can't sleep. I thought I'd go out and look at the stars for a bit." She forced a grin. "Better than counting sheep."

Annie ignored her comment, apparently satisfied with the answer and turned to her husband. "How long before you need to go get the man?"

"Should be a while. He has to dig up the coffin and we buried it six feet down, then pry it open and somehow move the corpse into the fancy new box." He almost shivered. "Can't say as I would like that job. Just think..." His voice faded as the two moved into the dining room.

Harriet slipped out the door and shoved her feet into her moccasins. Scooping up the mug, she tossed the dregs into the bush by the steps and shoved the mug inside her shirt. Mounting the steps intending to return to her room, she paused to tip her head back and admire the stars.

"Oh! You startled me." She hadn't heard the man approach, lost in her thoughts and watching the night sky.

"Shout if you see a flare go up by the cemetery. Man said he'd signal me when he was ready from me to come back." Shannon stood in the shadows by the door.

"I haven't seen anything. Surely you can't expect him signal so soon?" She edged by him.

"Probably not. But he's a queer duck." Shan stared off into the dark in the direction

179

of the burial plot, though it was too far away to see even in the daylight.

"Goodluck, then. I'm for bed." Harriet hurried across the floor and climbed the steps. Once in her room, she breathed a sigh of relief before pulling the paper out of her pocket in order to read it better. "Holy Mary, mother of God," she whispered while her eyes skimmed down the page. "This implicates the Blechers, the Frasers and some names I don't know, all involved in moving quantities of illegal liquor and beer. Looks like they make a run about twice a month. Here's an odd name, French I bet. Francois. I wonder if that's the man with the accent that Winnie heard? Although I suppose he could be English with a French name. Mark needs to see this, and quickly."

She flipped the paper over. There was something scribbled on the back in pencil, but the writing was so faint and smudged she couldn't make it out. Maybe in the morning in the daylight she would be able to make something out. Folding the paper carefully, she tucked it into the dust jacket of the book she was currently reading.

Harriet undressed and pulled on the shirt she slept in. She was exhausted but her mind refused to settle enough to allow her to sleep. Finally giving up, she lit the lantern, turned it low, and picked up her book.

The crunch of gravel under the wheels of the wagon roused Harriet who was dozing over the book fallen in her lap. Padding over to the window she peered out. Shan was heading off in the direction of the Mowat cemetery. She glanced at her watch astounded to see it was just barely past midnight. The grave was dug deep, she'd seen that with her own eyes at the funeral. Was it possible that the undertaker had singlehandedly managed to dig up six feet of earth and then lever the coffin out of the hole? She gulped down bile as another thought occurred to her. Please God the man hadn't left the original coffin in place and only removed Tom's body from the grave. The condition of the corpse at time of burial was advanced in its decomposition. Even though the body had been embalmed, the decay before that had been substantial. She shuddered. Determined to wait and see how long it took Shan to return, she blew out the lantern and dragged the chair to the window. She sat with her chin resting on her hand, elbow braced on the sill. It was just going on for a quarter to one when the creak of wheels and the crunch of broken foliage announced the men's return.

The muted conversation of the two men preceded their appearance in the ring of light by the lodge entrance. The new, much sturdier, coffin was laid crossways over the wagon, Churchill steadied with his hand as the procession came to a halt.

"Where is the best place to store this until morning?" Churchill looked toward the lodge.

"You'll not be bringing that thing into the lodge," Annie declared, appearing on the top step. "Let it lay where it is." She gave a tight laugh. "Not like he's going to up and ran off, is it?"

"It is hardly a secure arrangement," Churchill complained.

"'Tis only until dawn when we get you to the station for the morning train," Shannon attempted to placate the officious man. He reached both hands over his head and stretched until his back cracked.

"I don't like it. My instructions from the family were to not leave the casket unattended at any time." The man clasped his hands behind his back.

"It's not comin' in here." Annie barred the door.

"For a fee, I can roust out one of the boys what works here and have him sit with the coffin. Will cost you though," Shannon offered.

Harriet grinned. Trust Shan to find a way to make money out of the event. Her thought was realized in the next words from the man's mouth.

"There'll be a bill for the cartage I've provided. Do I send it to you or the Thomsons? If you're the one doin' the payin' I'd just as soon have the money in cash."

The undertaker sniffed and regarded the other man in the dim light. "You will need to send your bill for the cartage to the Thomsons, or whoever they have appointed as the executor of the estate. On the other note, if you can provide someone to guard the coffin, I suppose that will be sufficient."

The men went into the lodge and shortly, one of the raggedy boys who did odd jobs for the Frasers and others in the vicinity settled himself on the bottom step of the lodge. The night was wearing on, even the stars seemed dim, though there was no glimmer of light in the eastern sky. Harriet rose and limped across to the bed. Her leg was all pin-prickly from sitting in the same position so long. She fell into the bed and finally went to sleep.

* * *

Harriet was downstairs in time to see the tail end of the wagon bearing the casket disappearing. There was no sign of the boy who'd guarded it the rest of the night. It was time to go in search of Mark Robinson and show him the page she'd stolen from Annie's accounting book. Her path took her by the trail to the cemetery. Curiosity made her climb the hill to the tiny yard, the light wind stirring the branches of the huge birch tree guarding the graves. Outside of the white picket fence, which was much in need of repair, she stood looking down at the disturbed grave. There was no sign of the original coffin so she supposed it must still be at the bottom of the grave. Harriet frowned; the depression left by the disturbed earth seemed far too shallow for the undertaker to have dug down all six feet. She walked around the site, pondering what she saw. He must have put the material he dug out close to the grave so he could easily toss it back in to refill the hole, but there seemed to be little evidence of that. And, he was only one man working by lantern light, was it possible to exhume the body and place it in the new casket in the short amount of time Churchill had been gone? Something else to discuss with Mark when she found him. Uneasy suspicions circled in her mind. On one hand you could hardly fault the man for not wanting to transfer the decomposing body out of the hole and into the new casket, not to mention shifting all that earth by himself, but Tom...Tom deserved some dignity did he not? The dignity and comfort of being buried close to kin and home. Patting the pocket where the paper crackled she bent her head and said a quiet prayer for the repose of Tom's spirit, wherever he may be. With one backward glance, she left the cemetery and continued on her way.

Mark's ranger cabin was vacant when she arrived. Taking the opportunity to rest, she sat on the stump of a large tree damaged in a windstorm that Mark had sawed flat. She took the paper from her pocket and read it over a few times. The faint scribbling on the back was still indecipherable. She narrowed her eyes and turned the paper this way and that with no luck. Glancing at her watch she saw it was just after nine. If Mark wasn't back by nine-thirty, long after the morning train had departed, Harriet decided she would go back to the lodge and ask if anyone had seen him. That shouldn't arouse any suspicions, she and Mark often shared coffee and conversation. In the meantime, she tipped her head back and let the sun soak into her. The little sleep she'd managed hadn't done much to refresh her at all. At nine-twenty-five she got to her feet and considered leaving a note for Mark but was reluctant to enter his cabin as it felt like an invasion of his privacy. After a moment of indecision, she started back the way she had come. Rounding a curve in the trail she came upon the object of her journey.

"Miss St. George...Harriet! What a surprise to find you here," Mark greeted her.

"Hello, Mark. I've come to see about something rather important," Harriet informed him.

"Well then, come along back to the cabin and you can tell me over a cup of coffee."

"That seems splendid." She matched her steps to his and they soon arrived at the cabin.

"Come in, come in." Mark pushed the door open and ushered her inside. He stoked up the fire in the stove and set the coffee pot on top. "Shouldn't take too long for it to warm up. I made a pot this morning before I went to the station to meet the morning train."

"I'm in no hurry." Harriet sat at the small table.

"Curious thing though, at the station." Mark joined her.

"What was that?" She leaned her elbows on the table.

"There was an undertaker there with a casket waiting to be boarded. When I inquired about it, he said he was Mr. Churchill the Thomson family's undertaker come to take Tom home. That is something I should have been told about and there should have been permissions asked prior to the exhumation of the body. I must speak with William Bartlett, he's the park superintendent, about this. There was nothing to do but let the man have the casket loaded and board himself, but it is most unusual."

"Yes, I saw him at the lodge last evening. He had Shan take him and his casket out to the cemetery and then signalled him in some way to come and fetch him when he was done. It didn't seem to take as long as I expected, and I went by the grave this morning, you might want to take a look and see what you think," Harriet said.

"I'll do just that. I need to make sure things have been put back as they should." Mark got up and poured two mugs of coffee before returning to the table. "Now what was it you wished to discuss?"

Harriet pulled the paper out of her pocket and handed it to him. Mark read the information, then set his cup down and read it again. He raised his gaze to meet hers.

"This is mighty interesting. How did you come by it?"

"I might have found it in Annie's office." A flush heated her face.

"I see." He folded the paper. "Can I keep this?"

"Of course. The last thing I need is to be found in possession of it." Harriet leaned back in her chair. "I'm sure the people mentioned there had something to do with Tom's death."

"Why do you think that, Harriet? That's a serious accusation."

"Because Tom knew about the bootlegging, or at least some part of it, and he told me and Winnie he was going to come and speak with you about what he knew. Did that occur?"

"No, Tom did mention he needed to see me about something, but I never did find out what it was."

Harriet nodded. "That's what I was afraid of. I think someone found out that Tom was going to tell you what he knew about the operation, and they took pains to silence him."

"That's as may be, but what's on this paper won't help to prove your suspicions. I will take the information to the superintendent and let him deal with it, but we will need much more evidence to prove first that there was foul play, and second that any of these people were involved."

Harriet reached across and grabbed his hand in a most ungenteel manner. "But I know where there is evidence," she whispered.

"What do you mean?"

"I was investigating my suspicions and that led me to explore the Blecher's boathouse. You know they were the only ones who never searched the bush, like they expected to find Tom in the water, and I saw them towing something behind their boat near Little Wapomeo a few days before Tom was found. So, I was suspicious of them from the start, and you know also that Martin Junior had no love for Tom."

"I will ignore the fact you were trespassing for the moment. What did you find?"

"I found the missing paddle from the canoe. The favourite one Tom used to paddle all the time. It was hidden in the bow of the motor launch under a tarp."

"Are you sure it was Tom's paddle? One paddle can seem very much like another," Mark prodded her for more information.

"Yes, yes. I'm sure. I could recognize it anywhere. And there was blood stains on the thin edge of the paddle." Harriet let go of Mark's hand take a sip of coffee.

"How do you know it was blood? It could have been paint or stain," Mark reasoned.

"I'm sure, because while I was in the boathouse, Bessie and her brother came in—"

"They discovered you in the boathouse?" Mark was surprised.

"Almost." Harriet grinned. "I heard them in time, so I shoved everything back where it was and went into the water. I hid under the boardwalk that runs down the inside of the boathouse, so I heard everything they said.

"Which was?" Mark toyed with his mug, turning it round in his hands.

"Martin was worried was someone had been in the boathouse, but Bessie said it was fine, that their father had taken care of things. Martin Junior said people were asking questions and how they should never have said they found the canoe. Then he said how they had to get rid of the paddle, they should have left it with the canoe, and it was stupid to carry it away. Bessie said he knew why they kept it. The edge was all bloody and their father wasn't sure the lake would wash it all off. She said she tried to remove the blood but the stain wouldn't go away." Harriet let out the breath she'd been holding while she spoke. She'd been talking too fast to allow her to breathe.

"How did you get out?"

"I waited until they left, then swam out the open end and back to shore. I was very careful that no one saw me. Especially Mrs. Blecher, that woman scares the dickens out of me. Then I made my way back to the lodge."

"It was very dangerous what you did." Mark paused. "Did you bring the paddle away with you?"

Harriet shook her head. "No, at the time I was just thinking about getting out of there. I should have gone back for it, I suppose. Does it matter now?"

"I'm afraid it does. Without that paddle and where it is found, we have nothing to tie the Blechers, or anyone else, to Tom's death."

"So, we need the paddle." Harriet got to her feet.

"Don't be silly and go back there to retrieve it," Mark cautioned her. "They might well have gotten rid of it by now, and they must be worried that someone was snooping about, they might be being more diligent about watching the boathouse."

"Perhaps, but if I went in the same way I left, say in the dark, the chances they would see anything are slim."

"I still say it is an unnecessary risk, and I caution you to bide your time. Let me speak with Bartlett before you do anything."

"I suppose you are right." She glanced at her watch. "I have taken up enough of your time, Mark. I'll be on my way and let you get on with your day." Harriet took her leave and walked slowly back toward the lodge. Very undecided about what direction she should take now.

Chapter Thirteen

The next morning, Harriet took a biscuit and some coffee and went to sit on a large boulder by the lake. Her position was sheltered from view of the lodge or dock by a stand of cedar trees. Their lacy branches formed a lovely, scented swaying curtain the seemed to hold her in its embrace. *Dear Lord, she prayed, show me the way I should travel. Give me a sign. Should I sit and wait for Mark to set things in motion and give the Blechers, or whoever, time to get rid of the paddle, or should I try and get it myself?"*

Commonsense told her to wait for Mark, but the stronger inclination was to take matters into her own hands and try to retrieve the paddle herself. Listening to her impulses had gotten her into hot water in the past, so she should err on the side of caution, shouldn't she? Her mind said yes, her heart said no. Restless, she shifted on the sunny boulder, absently watching dragonflies flitting across the still, shallow water, occasionally alighting on a lily pad. It reminded her of the day she and Tom sat and watched them last summer and then later in the day, the ripples on the surface as fish came to the surface to feed. If people she knew were involved in Tom's murder, surely she owed it to her friend to pursue all the leads. A small shower of rocks plunged into the water about ten feet beyond where she sat concealed by the cedars. Harriet started to call out and ask who was there, then held her silence.

"The *kinder* are worried someone has been poking around the boathouse in particular. Martin fears someone suspects us of having something to do with the death," Martin Sr. spoke quietly, but the sound carried clearly to Harriet.

"They're just getting the heeby-jeebies, Martin. I don't think it has anything to do with Tom's death. It's more likely to do with the operation we're involved in," Shannon answered.

"Why do you think that is so?" Blecher sounded almost relieved.

"Annie thought someone had been nosing around in the office the other day. Her papers weren't in the same order as she left them, though how she could tell I'll never know. I didn't give it much thought at the time. You know how women can be...but if you agree with Martin and Bessie, that someone has been snooping in your motor launch, then maybe Annie was right. I'll get her to check if she thinks anything is missing."

"This could be trouble, *ja*?" Martin's voice rose a bit.

"Could be." A rasping sound told Harriet Shannon was rubbing his chin. "First thing is to find out just who it is that's been snooping...and then..."

"*Ja*, and then...?"

"And then take care of them." Shannon spat into the water not three feet from Harriet's place of concealment.

Now she was more relieved than ever she hadn't called out. She held her breath, almost afraid to breathe in case the men somehow heard her. Silly, of course, but adding this bit of information to what she'd already collected would make her discovery treacherous and put her in a very vulnerable position.

"What do I tell the *kinder*? Martin is very nervous, and we haven't worried Louisa too much with this, of course. You know how volatile she can be," Martin Sr. asked.

"Tell them to just stay put, don't do anything out of the ordinary. We might have to put off the next shipment for a week or so. Robinson has been sniffing around with some questions. He was some put out about the body being moved without him being notified first. I better let Francois know there might be a delay with the pickup at Tea Lake," Shan said.

"I will tell them, but I have to say Martin wants to get that cursed paddle out of the motor launch as soon as possible. I caught he and Bessie talking about throwing it into the bush on Little Wap or into the lake further down."

"Don't do anything that stupid! Someone is sure to see something, especially now we suspect someone has suspicions regarding us. Get control of your kids, Blecher," Fraser growled.

"*Ja, ja*, I agree. I will speak with them as soon as I return home." He stopped for a moment then continued. "What if it isn't the ranger, or that Trainor girl, or that other nosy parker who is always asking questions, they are the ones I thought of first, what if that brother, George, has hired a private investigator to inquire into his brother's death?"

"Could be, could be. There's that new guest just showed up a few days ago, says he's come up from Toronto hoping to paint with Thomson, said he hadn't heard about the tragedy. Some artist or another just come back from painting out west, 'least that's what he told Annie. I'll get Annie to go through his stuff when she's cleaning the room. You never can tell," Shan actually sounded worried.

The men's voices faded as they moved away. Harriet let out the breath she was holding and pried her trembling hands apart. *I assume I am the nosy parker always asking questions, it's too bad they suspect me, it may make things harder. Thank God I gave Mark that paper, now even if Annie or someone decides to search my room they'll find nothing. I must warn Mark to be careful as well. It worries me, the news that Martin and Bessie are talking about moving the paddle. I'm not sure Blecher Sr. can control them. Especially the brother, he's such a hot head...It might be best if I tried to get that paddle before they can do something with it.*

Harriet stayed perched on the boulder for another twenty minutes, then she slipped off and moved away from the lodge following a narrow trail that skirted the lake. There was no way she wanted to be seen coming from the direction where the two men had their discussion. The weight of suspicion, imagined or otherwise, hung over her like a cloud. A frisson of anxiety set her heart racing. Should she dare try for the paddle or take the safe course and wait for Mark. *For the love of God, I need to make up my mind before I drive myself crazy.* She followed the trail for a good half mile before pushing through the underbrush to access a wider deer trail she knew was up on a ridge. Sweating from the exertion and swatting at insects, she sauntered back toward the lodge in what she hoped was an innocent manner. When she came clear of the bush at the head of the trail she glanced about and was reassured to see the vicinity was vacant. Still moving in an unhurried way, she crossed the chip yard to the lodge and went inside. The hall was also empty, she noted the office door was closed and now sported a padlock.

Well, that's new. The wry thought crossed her mind as she made her way to her room.

* * *

Much later, she hiked over to the Trainor cottage hoping to find Winnie home.

"Harriet, I'm glad to see you. Come in," Winnie greeted her.

"I wasn't sure you were back yet." Harriet stepped inside and closed the screen door on the insects. "I see Louisa has put a new sign, tourist bothering her again? Or just her pleasant personality?"

Winnie giggled. "I don't think most locals pay much attention to it. Other than to marvel at how big she made the sign. I wonder if the bears can read 'No Trespassing' or if she'll chase them out with a broom like she does the tourists."

"Lord only knows." Harriet joined in the amusement, then sobered. "Is your father about?"

"Not at the moment, he's out trolling in the canoe hoping to land some trout."

"Did you get in touch with the Thomsons?"

"With some difficulty. I discovered the wires were down between Scotia and Huntsville when I got to Scotia Junction. It was around seven-thirty in the evening, and I was much vexed. Then I looked up the

Grand Trunk Railway agent and explained my situation. He was perfectly lovely about it all and sent the messages to Huntsville for me, all free of charge."

"Then what did you do?"

"I went and called on Mr. Churchill and asked him some plain questions. He was very adamant that I not use his name if I spoke of these things to anyone else. He seems a conscientious man and said he thought the bill from Flavelle was very steep. Because the man is not an undertaker, but only a furniture maker, he had to bring the embalmer from Sprucedale so that doubled the expense. I have no doubt that Shan will try and make a bit on top if he can when he presents the bills to the family. Mr. Churchill said the original casket was very rough, not painted, and I believe it had no handles. Heavens it wasn't even sealed properly, nor was it copper lined as it should have been. That may have been because the copper lining costs more than the coffin itself."

"So, George did ask this Churchill to come and being Tom back to Leith?" Harriet clarified.

"Oh yes, his sisters and family as most anxious for him to be brought home. I believe George planned to accompany the casket on its journey." Winnie wiped a bit of moisture from her cheek and sniffed. "I'm some glad he will be close to family, but I will always think of him as being here and I will keep that patch where he lay in our little cemetery looked after."

Harriet waited until Winnie gained control, then broached the delicate subject of the impending child. "Have you decided what to do about..." She nodded at the other woman's waist. "I can't even imagine how you are coping with that dilemma alongside Tom's death."

"I have contacted some relatives in the States. I plan to stay with them until after the baby is born...then I'm not sure what I will do."

"Does your father suspect anything?" Harriet chewed her bottom lip.

Winnie shook her head. "No, and I intend to leave before anyone can notice my condition." She reached across and gripped Harriet's hand. "I will miss you. I'll write, I promise. And I will leave my address with you. Do you know where you'll winter? I imagine returning to your father's house isn't an option."

Harriet snorted and patted her friend's hand. "I will never darken that doorstep again. I will most likely look for a room in Huntsville or Parry Sound. I have some friends in both places and hopefully I can find a job of some sort to keep me from going stir crazy."

"That's grand. I'm glad you've got a plan."

"When are you leaving for your relatives?"

"Tomorrow on the morning train. I've done what I can for Tom and his family, there's no point in putting things off."

"Winnie, what are you plans for after the child is born? Will you bring the baby back with you?"

"I haven't decided for certain, but I don't think I could bear being classed as an unwed mother. You know how cruel people can be, both to me and to a bastard child. My relatives have offered to take the child in and raise him or her as their own. I can't think of a better solution."

"But wouldn't it be a comfort to have a part of Tom still with you?" Harriet was having trouble coming to terms with giving up a child.

"Maybe it would, maybe it wouldn't. I don't know, but I do know a baby is no replacement for Tom. Could never be. What if I came to resent the child because he or she wasn't his or her father?"

"I suppose, but still..."

"I know it must seem harsh to you, but I just feel in my heart I wouldn't be a good mother. I've already made up my mind and my family in the States is expecting me."

"Will you ever tell your father?"

"Absolutely not. You are the only one who knows, and I trust you will never betray me."

"Of course, your secret is safe with me. Let me fill you in what I've discovered." Harriet went on to relate her foray into

Annie's office as well as the excursion to the Blecher boathouse and explain what she found.

"In the name of all the saints! I knew it, it just knew it! I never trusted that Martin Jr., no matter how he tried to sweet talk me. You say Mark Robinson is going to handle things, look into it?"

Harriet nodded. "That's what he told me."

"Is he going to search the boathouse and get that paddle. Oh, I wish I wasn't leaving so quickly. You must be sure to write and let me know how it turns out."

"He must speak with Superintendent Bartlett first, but then, yes he will handle things." Harriet assured her, not wishing to delay Winnie's intended departure. No good could come of her condition being discovered and the ensuant gossip and vitriol that would go with it. *One woman disowned at Canoe Lake this summer is enough.* The wry thought crossed Harriet's mind. She got to her feet and Winnie followed suit. The two women embraced and then stepped back.

"I will miss you, Winnie Trainor," Harriet said, blinking back tears.

"And I you, Harriet St. George," Winnie responded.

"I'll write," Harriet promised, heading for the door.

"I'll write back," Winnie replied, standing with her hands tangled in her skirts.

Harriet slipped out the door, forcing herself not to look back. She backtracked and skirted the Blecher two-story cottage which sat on the lot just south of the Trainor's. If no one was about perhaps she could slip into the boathouse and retrieve that thrice damned paddle. Ignoring the large and prominent No Trespassing sign, she wended her way thought the thick bush, keeping an ear out for any sign of life, human or otherwise. Harriet wasn't sure which she feared most, Louisa Blecher or a black bear intent on scavenging some food. Her heart stuttered at the sharp crack of a branch when she miss-stepped. *I must be nervous. I haven't been this noisy in the bush since I was a kid. Concentrate. Pay attention.*

The roof of the boathouse reared its head above the tall bushes clinging to the banks of the lake. Moving ever more cautiously, Harriet edged along the verge of the woods, approaching the structure from the side furthest from cottage whose white-washed walls shone through the screening greenery. One foot raised to step out of concealment and onto the narrow path, she shrank back into the safety of a fragrant cedar at the sound of the boathouse door creaking open. Holding her breath she peeked through the lacy branches. Martin Jr. and Louisa emerged from the doorway. Martin carried a large tool of some sort while his mother strode ahead of him toward the cottage.

"Come, Martin. Hurry." Louisa made a waving motion with her hand but did not look back.

He stopped long enough to pull the door shut and shove the lock home. Shaking his head and scowling he scurried after his mother. Harriet took a careful breath. Having held it so long without thinking that spots started dancing in her vision. There had been no sign of the paddle in either of the Blecher's hands, but the darn door was locked now. The only way in would be from the lake.

Defeated for the moment, Harriet wended her way back to the trail that would return her to the lodge. With some planning it would be possible to sneak in and get the paddle once the night set in. *It's not the best plan, but it's the only one I have at the moment.* Seething with impatience, she reached the lodge and went inside. The murmur of voices came from the area where the Fraser's private rooms were. Her moccasined feet made no sound on the wooden boards of the floor. The entry hall was vacant so the other guests must be out and about. There was no one to remark on the fact she crept over to the far side of the hall, pressing close to the frame of the slightly ajar door.

"There's nothin' to worry about. Your Martin is shying at shadows," Shan was saying.

"*Nein*. I am also sure that someone has been asking questions that they shouldn't," Blecher Sr. said.

"Who would that be?" Annie inquired as though she already knew the answer.

Harriet pressed closer to the wall, hardly daring to breathe in case she missed any nuance of speech that might indicate she was in danger.

"Hugh's daughter, if it's anyone. That one just won't let things lie. Contacting Tom's family, causing all that fuss," Shan said. "From what I've heard from Geroge Thomson she's been casting doubt about my honesty."

"*Ja*, that one I found lurking by the boathouse just yesterday," Martin Sr. said. "Louisa caught her and chased her off with the broom."

"Wish I'd seen that." Annie giggled.

"Was she in the boathouse?" Shan sounded a bit worried now.

"*Nein*. Louisa thought not."

"The item was still where it's supposed to be?" Annie inquired.

"*Ja, ja.*" Blecher sounded impatient. "The ranger's been around more than usual too. It is possible he is suspicious as well."

"He'll keep to his own business if he knows what's good for him," Shan growled.

"What's the plan to get rid of the...item? It's pure stupidity to leave it where it can be found and point the finger at any one of us." Annie declared.

"I have the plan."

Harriet sucked in a breath. *That's a new voice. He sounds French, I wonder if this is the mysterious Francois Winne saw. Go on, go on. What's the plan?*

"It better be good," Shan warned. "Things are getting too hot."

"*Oui*, and the big men are getting very impatient with the delays. It is not good to anger them," the French man said.

"*Nein, nein*. We must make them happy. I have heard stories of what happens to those who annoy them," Blecher actually sounded worried, his tones edged with fear. "I have made promises, promises we dare not break."

"Fine mess you've got us into," Annie snarled. "Shan, you said there wasn't any risk, just some easy money."

"Shut up, woman. Let me take care of this," Shan growled back.

Heavy footsteps followed by a door slamming deeper in the lodge suggested Annie had stomped off in a fit of anger.

"What is your plan?" Blecher said, a chair scraped as if the man had stood up.

Harriet hovered, wondering if she should get clear before she was discovered, but the temptation to hear more held her in place.

"After dark, I will come and get the item. It will disappear forever, and no one will be the wiser. Certainly not some nosy woman or that excuse for a park ranger. Have it ready for me. I won't wait around for it," the French man ordered.

"You can take care of that? Wait for Francois in the boathouse until he comes," Shannon addressed Blecher.

"*Ja, ja*. Either myself or Martin Jr. will be there," he assured the two men.

"Better you do it. The son, he is jumpy. I don't trust him," Francois said. "If anything is suspicious I will disappear, and you will be left with getting rid of the item yourselves. And answer to anyone the big men send to see why there are delays. You will not like these men, I promise you."

"I will be there. There is no need to contact your *big men*. It will be done as you ask," Martin Sr. said with some truculence. He obviously didn't like being ordered about.

"See that it is. Now, I go. Tonight, I see you after full dark. No lights, you understand?" Francois snapped out the words.

"No need to get testy, Francois. We'll take care of things on our end, so long as you can assure that things are taken care of on yours," Shan attempted to defuse the volatile situation that was threatening to develop between the other two men.

Francois made a guttural French sound before he spoke. "I go."

The sound of chairs scraping on the rough floor and accompanying footsteps sent Harriet scurrying for the stairs. She was on the second step when Annie spoke.

"Miss St. George," the tone was stiff and officious, "I didn't see you come in just now, and I was just cleaning up in the dining room, you weren't there either." Annie stood with hands jammed on her hips, brows drawn down over her eyes.

"Oh! Well, you must have missed me then. I just came in and was on my way up to my room to fetch my paints. I thought to try and catch the sunset, it lights up the trees across the lake and the colours reflected in the water are perfect right now. I need to hurry before the light changes." Harriet threw the words over her shoulder and bounded up the steps. Once in her room, she leaned on the closed door and pressed a hand to her chest to still her galloping heart.

Oh, dear God. Did she see me listening at the door? But she couldn't have, could she? There must be a back way into the dining room from their quarters, she sure didn't come into the hall, I would have been discovered for certain. I'm just being paranoid. There's no way they could have known I was there.

She slipped the lock on the door and moved to sit on the edge of the bed. Once her heart slowed, she put on a flannel shirt over the lighter one she was wearing and gathered up her paintbox. Now she'd have to make a show of going out to paint the God-blessed sunset or Annie would be even more suspicious. The thought of changing her moccasins for boots crossed her mind, but if she was going to have to enter the boathouse later from the lake, moccasins were easier to slip out of. Given the conversation she'd overheard, she needed to get into the boathouse and retrieve the paddle before Martin Sr. went down to wait for the French man and certainly before this Francois ever showed up. There was something very dangerous about that man and Harriet had no desire to meet him face to face.

On her way down the stairs she made sure to thump on each step and bang the paintbox off a few spindles in the railing. Annie came out of the office as Harriet crossed the floor toward the outside door.

"I'm off to catch the sunset," Harriet called without pausing.

Annie watched her leave in silence, but Harriet didn't like the expression on the woman's face. Sour as always but was it her imagination or was there something more she should be worried about. *Nothing I can do about it now. I need to get the canoe and set out as if nothing is out of the ordinary. Lord, I wish Winnie were still here. I could use the company, not to mention a lookout.*

Once in the canoe, Harriet paddled away from Mowat. She rounded Big Wap and let the vessel drift with the gentle current. *Now what? There's time to kill before I dare try to get the paddle. I suppose I should produce a painting or two to prove to Annie that I wasn't lying about what I was up to.* The lake was calm and, in the lee of the big island, where she sat close to the shore, the canoe lay motionless. It took only a matter of minutes for her to set up the paintbox and put brush to palette. She lost herself in the glorious scene before her. The westering sun threw long slanted beams of golden light across the water and lit the trees on the eastern side of the lake as if with a spotlight. Each needle of spruce and pine and each leaf was limned in honeyed light. As she painted the sky changed from eggshell blue to a deeper sapphire, the light softened, and motes of dust and pollen danced in the cooling air. Behind her, the western sky was awash in scarlet and magenta, tinged to orange and saffron at the edges. Soon, the colours reflected in the still lake. Harriet let the brush hang idle in her fingers, her heart singing with the beauty and serenity that was unfolded before her. *I wish Tom were here to see this.* The thought tightened her throat and broke her out of her reverie. Dusk was falling, enfolding the lake with shadows and mist.

Harriet took stock of the work she'd accomplished and allowed that it was very satisfactory. Perhaps that friend of Tom's what was his name? Dr. MacCallum from

Toronto, he was the one who took care of marketing Tom's work. With any luck he might be willing to at least look at her paintings. Packing the wet paintings carefully, she closed up the paintbox and stowed it in its customary place. It was just coming full dusk, if she was going to try and beat the men to the paddle, now was the time. Kneeling behind the middle thwart of the canoe, she dipped her paddle into the water and with the practiced stroke of a master canoeist, moved across the lake leaving only a faint ripple and no sound besides the quiet lap of the water against the canvas side of the vessel.

She rounded Little Wap and hugged the shore intent on reaching her goal. Hardly daring to breath, she nudged the canoe into a tiny cove and climbed out onto the granite boulders at the shoreline. Securing the painter to a convenient brush with a quick release knot, she considered her options. It was earlier enough; she should be able to nip into the boathouse and get out before the Blechers finished their evening meal. Even better if the door was conveniently unlocked. Pulling a dark cap low over her face, Harriet wriggled through the bush and approached the shadowy structure from the side away from the cottage. No light glimmered through the grimy windowpane, so luck was with her so far. Slipping from one cluster of shadow to the next, she reached the structure and stepped out onto the path. Her fingers encountered the padlock which she turned over in her palm, feeling for the shackle in the dark. Whoever locked the door last failed to be sure the pin engaged, and the shackle popped free when she pulled.

Her breath caught in her throat. *Luck or a trap? I'm not sure what to do now. I think I'd feel better if it was locked up tight as a drum.* She faded back into the underbrush and took a deep breath to steady her resolve. *In for a penny, in for a pound as Aunt Lois used to say. Here I go.* Harriet moved back to the door and unhooked the padlock, leaving it hanging on the hasp. The interior of the building was dark, little light filtering in through the dust accumulated on the tiny window. She edged past the tools and equipment on the workbenches and along the boardwalk beside the motor launch. Hesitating beside the craft, Harriet listened for any trace of sound coming from outside. Nothing stirred except the haunting call of the loons and a couple of whippoor-wills calling to each other. She stepped down into the boat, cursing under her breath as the weight made the water lap against the hull and the sides of the boathouse. Still no sign of anyone coming to interrupt her activity.

Her toe caught on something, and she smothered an oath. *Careful. Be more careful.* It was only a few more feet to the canvas laying under the deck covering the bow area. She ducked under and lifted the canvas. *Yes! It's still here. Now to get it and get out of here.* Closing her fingers over the shaft of the paddle, she pulled it out, grimacing at the sound of it scraping across the canvas. She trembled so hard she worried it would rock the boat. Harriet forced herself to take three deep breaths and then began to back out from under the deck. On hands and knees, she was almost clear when the sound of voices made her freeze.

"It's almost dark and there's no moon right now. It should be perfect for our purposes," Martin Sr.'s voice echoed a bit for some reason.

"*Oui*, excellent," the Frenchman replied.

"Martin must have left the door unlocked again. I will speak with him," Blecher's voice sounded oddly complacent rather than annoyed. There was a rattle as the padlock was removed and the door creaked open.

Harriet's gut clenched. Using the sound of the men's entry, she moved as far back into the nose of the bow as she could and pulled the tarp over herself. The paddle was lying uncovered in front of her hiding place. At the moment getting out of the boathouse in one piece was more important than the paddle. She made herself as small as possible and barely breathed, hating the faint rasping of the canvas each time she took a breath. Her heart was pounding so hard it seemed impossible that the two men couldn't hear it thundering away. There was the sound of a match striking, she peeked around the edge of the canvas. The man's face she'd seen meeting with Shan and others was thrown into stark relief in the tiny flare of light. Biting her lip, Harriet tucked her chin in, she remembered Tom saying how your eyes could give you away by glinting in any source of light if you were hunting.

The two men conversed in tones too low for her to catch the words. They seemed content to stand about, as if they were waiting for something...or someone. *It was a trap! They just don't know I'm here already. With any luck they'll give up waiting, take the paddle and leave. Please God.* Time moved oddly for Harriet. She felt she'd been hiding for hours and yet somehow she knew it wasn't that long. Another match flared and feet shifted on the rough boards.

"I think we've waited enough time," Blecher said.

"That Fraser woman may have been wrong and painter woman didn't hear anything. We've been wasting our time," Francois declared. "You know how women are, imagining all sorts of things. Phah!"

"*Ja, ja.* I worry though, my Louisa also caught her snooping around, but she was gone before Louisa could confront her," Blecher replied.

"Once the paddle is gone there is nothing to worry about. There will be nothing to connect any of us to what happened out on the lake. It would have been much better if the body had never surfaced, though," Francois remarked.

"The copper fishing line should have held, but there must have been some silk line which came loose. *Ja*, it would have been less trouble if he had just disappeared," Blecher agreed. After a long pause he spoke again. "How did it happen? Such a strong man, how did you get the best of him?"

Oh ho! Now this is interesting, Harriet thought.

"You sure you wish to know this thing? If I tell, you must never speak of it or you will find yourself joining this man," Francois spoke with quiet conviction, leaving no doubt he meant what he said.

"*Ja*, maybe best I don't know." Blecher's voice trembled a tiny bit under his American-German accent.

The Frenchman gave an expansive sigh followed by the rustle of material. "I tell you anyway. Then I have the knowledge you won't speak. I borrow one of the Algonquin canoes, they not miss it, then I come to lake here and launch. I go out near islands, out of sight of the buildings. I wait and I make plans. If one does not work, the others will. Always. The man come around the little island and I pretend to be in trouble. He come to me. I am near island in shallow water. He stick out his paddle, thinking perhaps I am stuck on a sunken log, I don't know. I grab the paddle and take it from him, before he can shout, I hit him on the side of the head. Very hard with the edge. He fall, almost tip canoe. I grab him, blood is coming from ear. That strike never fails me. He has the convulsion, then stop breathing. I make sure, before I drag him into deeper water, away from island. I wrap leg in fishing line, tie to rock, and sink him. Then it is done. I am professional, I do my job well. I tip canoe over, push it out into the channel and leave it there for someone to find. Look like accident."

"Except a lot of people don't believe it was an accident," Blecher protested. "And the body didn't stay down."

Cloth rustled and Harriet assumed the Frenchman shrugged. "Sometimes it happens, but it took long enough that no one can connect me to anything. No one saw me with him."

"*Nein*, instead they think we had something to do with it," Martin accused the man.

"That, my friend is your problem," Francois told him.

The scent of cigarette smoke floated down to where Harriet huddled. Her heart shuddered in her chest. *I knew Tom didn't just slip and fall. I knew it. I've got to get out of here and tell Mark. All because they thought he was going to mess up their little scheme.* It was all she could do not to burst out of her hiding place and scream at the two men. *Calm yourself, Harriet. That won't accomplish anything and it's a good way to end up like Tom.* She swallowed the bile rising in her throat. The beginnings of panic tightening her chest.

The knowledge she now possessed made her anxious to escape the boathouse. Were they going to stand around all night? Her legs were cramping from kneeling on them, and she was lightheaded from trying to breathe under the musty canvas. Not to mention the smell of liquor that permeated the material. *I don't know how much longer I can keep this up, but what is the alternative. Stay strong, Harriet. Stay strong.*

"What is taking so long?" Louisa's voice cut through the men's muted conversation.

"We are waiting a while longer to see if the woman will show up. Go back to the house, if she sees anyone around you'll scare her off," Martin ordered his wife.

"Just hurry up and get done what needs to be done. Next thing you know that ranger will be showing up," Louisa grumbled. The door creaked open and shut as she left.

"She might be right. It is getting late, and I think if the woman was coming she would have been here by now," Blecher said, clearly growing impatient.

"Go and get the thing then and I'll be gone," Francois said. The glowing end of a cigarette flicked through the dark and fizzled as it hit the water.

The boat rocked as someone stepped in. Harriet clutched the canvas tighter, worried it would slip enough to reveal her hiding place.

"This is strange," Martin sounded puzzled and more than a bit worried.

"What is it?" Francois also came into the boat.

"The paddle is lying out in the open. I can't believe my son left it like that, not with how nervous he has been of late."

"Does it matter? Grab the thing and give it to me." Francois was clearly annoyed and ready to be done with the whole affair.

Blecher hesitated, one hand on the canvas and then shook his head and picked up the paddle. "Here, take it. Wipe off anything that could connect us with it," Martin straightened up and turned toward the stern.

Harriet allowed her shoulders to relax just a tiny bit. *Maybe I'll get out of this unscathed after all. Just go! Take the paddle and go!* She peeked over the edge of the canvas again. Martin had his back to her holding out the paddle, the Frenchman took it and shoved it in a sack he produced out of the inside of his jacket. The boat rocked when he jumped out onto the walkway. Martin stumbled and almost fell, cursing under his breath in German. A hand on the gunwale to steady him, the man stood on one of the seats and heaved himself up onto the relative stability of the walkway.

"I will be glad when all this is behind us and we can go back to our normal ways," Blecher said.

"As will I, although I'm not sure things will go back to what you say is normal," Francois said.

"What is the meaning of that?" Blecher demanded.

"The big men are not happy with you or the situation here. They have ordered me to make things right, which I will, and more importantly, I do not wish them to become unhappy with me," Francois growled.

"Meaning? Make yourself clear," Blecher sounded less sure of himself now.

"There is talk we may have to make different arrangements for future deliveries. We will see. I cannot speak for the big men. I only follow orders and relay their messages." In spite of the accent, the man's voice was flat and menacing.

"You threaten me and mine?" Martin sounded ready to do battle.

"We do not threaten, we promise. You would be wise to remember that."

"Do not threaten my family. We are not without ways to protect ourselves," Martin spoke boldly.

"Calm yourself. There is no need for harsh words at this time. If things settle down, perhaps they will decide to continue as things are. I am only the messenger."

"*Ja, ja.*"

The men moved toward the door much slower than Harriet wanted. It was going to take a few minutes before her legs would hold her. The pins and needles had long since passed into numbness and she knew from experience the sensation of feeling returning would not be pleasant.

The door burst open, just as she was sure they men were on the way out. *Oh for the love of God. Now what? Just go!* Desperation coloured her thoughts.

"What is the meaning of this?" Martin thundered.

The younger Blecher bent over his knees gasping for breath. "*Vater*...I came as fast as I could...I found a canoe tied up down in that small cove just past our cottage."

"Whose was it?" Francois took over the conversation.

"The woman from the lodge. You know the one," Martin Jr. huffed out the words, still trying to catch his breath.

"Hugh's daughter?" Martin Sr. broke in.

"No, the other one. Her friend."

"*Sacrebleu*," Francois cursed. "This we do not need."

"Did you see anyone between there and here?" Martin Sr. again.

"No, no one."

"She must be somewhere nearby. You, go get that canoe. We will find this woman and she must be taken care of," Francois ordered the younger Blecher who fled the boathouse with a wild-eyed backward look at his father.

"Taken care of how? I want no more on my hands," Martin Sr. declared.

"You do not need to know this thing. Now go and search for the woman. She is hiding close by, and she must not escape us. Go!" Francois shoved the man in the shoulder blades.

Harriet huddled deeper into the canvas. There was steel behind the Frenchman's words. *Take care of her, he said. I don't like the sound of that at all...* She suppressed a shudder. If the man would just leave, even for five minutes, she could force her legs to work and flip into the water and swim away into the darkness. They'd never find her, and she'd be gone before morning. Once she made it as far as the train station she'd be safe enough and would leave a sealed message with the station master or his wife for Mark. He would take it from there, she was sure. There'd be a seat on the morning train, and she'd go east toward Golden Lake. They'd expect her to go west to Sprucedale, throw herself on her father's mercy. *Now, that is never going to happen. I'll go to the Eady's. They were friends of Great Aunt Lois, they'll take me in.* With a rudimentary plan in place, Harriet was a little more confident she could escape. Now if only the Frenchman would get out of the boathouse... The loss of her canoe was a sore spot, but losing the canoe was a darn sight better than getting hurt herself. Let Fraser worry about the disappearance of the rented canoe.

The door creaked open again, followed by a rush of fresh air. "I've looked everywhere, I can't find her," Martin Jr. sounded panicked.

"Go and look again, in the water, up trees. She must know she has been found out by now," Francois ordered.

"She is nowhere near the cottage or boathouse," Martin Sr. joined them. "Maybe she got nervous and ran away when she saw us here ahead of her."

"Maybe, maybe not," Francois' tone was thoughtful. "We will see. Go, keep looking. She must be found."

"I want no more killing. It is enough," Martin Jr. said.

"Phah, you have no stomach for what is necessary and yet you ask me to introduce you to the big men," Francois sounded disgusted with the whole conversation.

"What is this? You wish to meet with the boss men in New York?" Martin Sr. growled. "What foolishness. You cannot return to the States until the war is over, and I forbid you to become involved with anything dangerous. You are my only son."

"It is of no matter. This thing I will not do. Now go and find that woman. I need to be gone." Francois shooed them out the door.

The door opening and closing followed the tramp of feet on the boards echoed in the building. Harriet listened hard, trying to ascertain if all the men left. Silence fell over the interior, broken only by the light slap of waves against the building and the bow of the boat. The vessel rocked gently, which told Harriet the wind must have come up quite a bit and ruffled the surface of the lake. Were they all gone? She was afraid to move and reveal herself if only two of the men had left. *I can't stay here all night either though, can I? Where's your courage, girl? Where's your gumption? You can't stay hidden like a 'fraidy cat forever.* Harriet attempted to bolster her confidence. Mere seconds would see her out of hiding and over the side into the water. Easy peasy, as Great Aunt Lois would say. She wished you could see her watch. It was hard to determine how much time had passed since the men left. If she waited too long they were sure to come back. I'll wait another little bit. I'll count to one hundred twice and then I'm going, she decided. The counting occupied her thoughts and calmed her somewhat. Reaching one hundred for the second time, she took a breath and peered out of the canvas covering her.

The interior was dim, the tool bench and things on it were hulking shadows that might hide the figure of man lurking in the area. Or not. The shadows shifted with the movement of the trees outside blown by the wind. Fear and indecision kept her where she was for a moment longer. Cautiously, she pushed the canvas away, wincing at the rasping of the tarp against itself. If anyone was nearby just outside, surely they would hear it. She froze in place and listened over the beat of her heart in her ears. Nothing moved, the door stayed closed. Harriet slipped to the edge of where the deck over the bow started, kneeling on the canvas still, she waited for her legs to get some feeling back in them. Still nothing moved in the building and no sounds came from outside other than bushes scraping against the side of the boathouse. Maybe they'd given up searching for her. Could her luck be that good? On hands and knees, Harriet poked her head out of the cover of the deck. Wriggling past the steering mechanism, she slid onto the bench seat and put out a hand to grasp the walkway and keep the boat from rocking and making enough noise to give her away if someone was waiting outside. So far, so good.

She fought the urge to shake her legs to get the sensation back, afraid to wait any longer, she took a breath and slung a leg over the side of the boat. There was just enough room for her to slip into the water between the boat and the walkway. Her foot was in the water up to the ankle and she shifted in order to swing her other leg over the side.

"What have we here?" A hand grasped her collar and hauled her back into the boat.

Harriet muffled a scream; it would do her no good and waste her energy. She struggled against the man holding her, who twisted the material of her shirt tight against her throat. The man grunted as her elbow found a home in his stomach and he shook her hard enough to snap her head back and forth. Harriet turned her head and attempted to bite anything she could get her teeth on. A sharp blow to her ear sent lights dancing in her vision.

"What do you want? she managed to croak out.

"I have what I want. For you to come out of hiding, *n'est pas*?" Francois sounded supremely pleased with himself.

With a one armed heave he hauled Harriet out of the boat and shoved her against the side of the building. Desperate, and with strength born of fear, Harriet kicked him in the shins, she was aiming much higher, but he wisely kept himself safe from that particular tactic.

"You would be wise to not try that again. I have little patience when it comes to women. They are good for only one thing."

His words instilled a new fear in her heart. The hold on her throat lessened and he struck a match with one hand.

"Ah, *oui*. It is as I suspected. The troublesome woman with the many questions." He peered into her face before dropping the match in the water. "You are a complication."

"I just wanted to see if Tom's paddle was left in the boat when they pulled the canoe in. I...I wanted to keep it to remember Tom

223

by. I meant no harm," Harriet tried to lie her way out the situation.

Francois laughed but there was no humour in it. "You think I would believe this?"

"It's the truth," she insisted. She slid down the wall to land on her bottom, the hold on her collar still restricting her breathing. Her fingers scrabbled on the boards looking for anything she could use as a weapon. "Why else would I be here?"

"You could not just ask the people who own the boat if they found the paddle?" Francois toyed with her.

Harriet shrugged as best she could. "They are not easy people to approach," she said.

"Neither am I," Francois tightened his hold and stepped on her hand that she'd inched toward his ankle hoping to trip him into the water or the boat.

She bit her lip and refused to acknowledge the pain in her hand. "Just let me go. I'll forget about the paddle. Winnie will be looking for me by now, I was supposed to meet her a long time ago. I wanted to give the paddle to Winnie..." Her words fell on stoney ground, and she let them trail off.

"The story changes." He dragged her to her feet, twisting one arm behind her and increasing the pressure on her windpipe. "The Trainor woman left earlier today, I saw her on the trail, you think I do not keep track of such things? To the train she went. If you wish to keep breathing you will do as I say."

"Just let me go. I won't say anything about anything," Harriet tried to reason with him.

"And I have a bridge in Brooklyn to sell you. I am not that stupid. I know you have been hiding all this time, before we arrived. You have heard far too much. Now move." Francois shoved her forward.

She stumbled as much as she could manage in an attempt to slow him down, but if she lost her footing he just dragged her until she got upright again. *Where are the Blechers? Hugh is away, Winnie's gone. They are my only hope and I'm afraid it's a pretty slim one.* They came out of the bush onto the narrow trail that ran between the cottages and Mowat. A wagon drawn by a shaggy pony waited by the side of the trail. Harriet's head swam from the blow to her head and doubled over as a fist impacted on her kidneys. By the time she could breathe again, her hands were tied behind her and then also tied to the ropes around her ankles. She grunted at the impact of hitting the floor of the wagon. Her mouth firmly bound so the only sounds she could make were muffled shouts that didn't carry any distance. The wagon bumped into motion. She blinked her eyes trying to figure out which way they were travelling by looking at the stars. Back toward the lodge, if her astronomy was correct. *Then what? Turn me over to the tender mercies of someone else. Maybe those big men he was talking about? I don't think I want to wait around for that.* She wriggled toward the open end of the wagon. If she could just get off and worm her way into the deep bush, she might have a chance of finding something sharp enough to break the ropes binding her. Halfway to her goal, she jerked to a halt with a strangled shriek. The fist grasping her hair yanked her back into her original position, pulling some of her hair out by the roots. Harriet subsided for a few moments blinking back tears from the burning of her scalp.

"Do not be trying that again," Francois warned her. For good measure he reached behind him and slapped her bringing the tears she'd refused to shed earlier coursing down her cheeks.

Where are we? There's nothing here... The wagon came to a stop. Francois jumped out of the driver's seat and came around to the open end of the wagon. He took hold of Harriet's feet and yanked her toward him. Once he had her upright, he slung her over his shoulder and moved toward the shelter of the close grown trees. His shoulder dug into her midriff making breathing difficult. Her scalp still stung and a trickle of something ran down her cheek. Sweat? Blood? At the moment Harriet didn't care. If the man would just put her down maybe she could head bunt him, or drive her shoulder into him and knock him down...

The man came out of the bush onto a narrow trail and turned up it. He grunted a bit as the land rose under his feet. A lightning blasted pine tree snag came into Harriet's peripheral vision, and she suddenly knew where she was. This was the trail to the Mowat cemetery. Where they'd buried Tom and where he had been exhumed. Fear threatened to turn her bowels to water. The place was a bit creepy even in the middle of the day. The big birch tree seemed to hover over the two graves, keeping watch and warning that no one should disturb the rest of those souls buried there. Most locals said it was hogwash, but Great Aunt Lois' mother was a Campbell and Aunt Lois claimed she had the second sight. The ability to see the future, and to see ghosts at times. Harriet shuddered and earned herself a painful pinch on her leg.

"Be still or I will drag you up here by your hair," Francois growled. He struggled up the last few feet of incline and dumped her on the ground near the spreading branches of a large spruce tree.

Harriet lay where she was dropped, frantically trying to wriggle her wrists through the ropes. The Frenchman wiped the sweat from his forehead and drew something small out of his jacket. He seemed to be contemplating something, and she lay quite still, not wishing to draw his attention. *Maybe he'll just leave me here and hope the bears or wolves will take care of things for him*. Francois rummaged in a different pocket and did something with the thing in his hand. It was dark under the trees and Harriet couldn't' make out what he was doing. At the back of her mind her common sense was telling her just what was happening but somehow her rational brain refused to believe it.

Francois held the long nosed pistol up and screwed something onto the muzzle. He leaned over Harriet. The lips curved in a smile that didn't reach his eyes. She'd seen that look in the eyes of a rattlesnake she'd come across last summer. "No one will even hear this, *ma petite*. Thanks to Hiram Maxim's little invention." He stroked the extension on the gun.

Harriet shook her head and attempted to spit out the gag. Her pulse raced, the rush of blood in her ears almost overwhelming the man's words. Digging her heels into the soft earth she pushed herself back under the protection of the tree until she was pressed up against the resinous trunk. Dead needles showered over her brought loose by her progress. *Dear God in heaven, help me*. In her terror she lost whatever words she was planning on praying next and she stared wide-eyed through the screen of sweeping branches. Her head and shoulders scraped down the trunk and hit the bed of needles when Francois grasped her ankles and yanked her out.

"You can run but you can't hide," his voice sing-songed. "Any last words?" He laughed. "I guess not, then." He brought the pistol up in his hand.

Harriet shook her head as hard as she could manage, tears leaking down her face into the gag. *He isn't actually going to use it, he's just scaring me so I'll keep my mouth shut. Someone will hear the shot and come looking...or maybe that's what that thing on the end of the pistol is for? It can't just end this way. It can't...*

The man moved suddenly, looming over her in the shadow of the spruce. There was a flash and bang simultaneously and then the world went black. His voice followed her down into the darkness.

"Say goodnight, sweetheart."

Epilogue

Yes, I know what you're thinking. I do. I should have left well enough alone and let Mark handle things. But hindsight is twenty-twenty as they say and here I am. I suppose there are worse places to spend eternity. It didn't hurt. That surprised me at first. I sat in the branches of the spruce looking down at what used to be me. Other than the gaping hole in the side of my head, I looked oddly peaceful, which was comforting in a strange sort of way. I must have turned my head when he fired, so at least my face in intact. As if that matters.

That was a long time ago and I've come to terms with what happened. My only regret is that I can never tell anyone what really happened. Only you, gentle reader. The Frenchman buried me under the spruce, digging through the roots into the sandy soil. He covered the evidence of his activities with leaves and needles. Not far from where the disturbed earth showed where Tom was buried and presumably exhumed. And here I have stayed.

The huge birch tree guards me from the little cemetery and seems friendly now, not menacing at all. The large spruce tree hovers over my resting place. I imagine that Tom is here still as well. Perhaps not his body; but given my suspicions that he may still lie under that crooked white cross just outside the fence, certainly his soul lingers here in the place he loved best.

If you haven't guessed by now, I'm dead. Or at least my spirit has left my earthly remains, but it appears I am still here. Perhaps I am not ready to go on yet, or perhaps it is because I feel I am already in heaven here on the lake I love so much surrounded by the woods I cherish. If you're thinking someone will be questioning where I have gone, the gossip going around is that I had a change of heart, packed up and left in the middle of the night and went off to merry old England to marry that fop Featherswallow my father trotted out. I hear the gossip of course, you know how sound travels across the water. Certainly, my family, especially my father, will not be inquiring as to my whereabouts and my sister, Amelia, is too firmly under Father's thumb to ever dare go against his wishes, so no one will be looking for answers. I suppose I'm okay with that. He buried me in the dark of the moon quite near to where Tom was originally buried. And so, there I will lie for all eternity, while my spirit goes where it will, visiting my old haunts, painting ghostly sketches, and paddling my canoe as the mists rise from Canoe Lake. I wonder if Winnie will join us when she passes? I'm sure her heart will always be here where she was so happy with Tom.

So, if you're out on Canoe Lake in the early morning or near dusk, you might see two canoes paddling across the still water, a man and a woman, but too far away to see clearly through the mist rising from the water, it just might be me and Tom. Perhaps, someone will recognize our canoes when you relate this experience. We'll raise a paddle to you in acknowledgement and then slip back into the mists.

The End

Research Sources

Klages, Gregory The Many Deaths of Tom Thomson Dundurn Press Toronto 2016

Clemson, Gayle I. Algonquin Voices Trafford Publishing 2007

Death on a Painted Lake url below https://canadianmysteries.ca/sites/thomson/portraits/artistspatrons/indexen.html

2023 Bestselling Author
Nancy M. Bell

Nancy lives in Castor, Alberta with her husband and various critters. She is a member of the Writers Guild of Alberta and board secretary of the Canadian Authors Association. Nancy has presented at the Surrey International Writers Conference, at the Writers Guild of Alberta Conference, When Words Collide and Word on the Lake. She has served as judge for the Writers Guild of Alberta – Alberta Literary Awards-YA Category. She has publishing credits in poetry, fiction, and non-fiction. Her work has been included in Tamaracks Canadian Poetry for the 21st Century, Vistas of the West Anthology of Poetry and The Beauty of Being Elsewhere. Her poetry is also being included by the University of Holguin Cuba in their Canada Cuba Literary Alliance (CCLA) program. The self published Touchstone was reviewed in A Shower of Warm Light by Prof. Miguel Angel Olive

Iglesias. Nancy is an avid horsewoman and a retired equestrian coach. She enjoys fostering rescue animals and gardening.

I have been a member of The Canadian Authors Association since August of 2021. Prior to that I was a member of The Writers Union of Canada for six years and often volunteered with them. I am also a member of The League of Canadian Poets.

She is at https://bookswelove.net/bell-nancy/

*Pl*ease visit her webpage
http://www.nancymbell.ca

You can find her on Facebook at
http://facebook.com/NancyMBell

More Books by this author from BWL Publishing Inc.

Canadian Historical Brides Collection
His Brother's Bride ~ Ontario
Landmark Roses – writing as Marie Rafter
On A Stormy Primeval Shore with Diane Scott
Lewis

Canadian Historical Mysteries Collection
Discarded ~ Manitoba

The Cornwall Adventures
Laurel's Quest ~ Book One
A Step Beyond ~ Book Two
Go Gently ~ Book Three

The Alberta Adventures
Wild Horse Rescue ~ Book One
Dead Dogs Talk ~ Book Two
Chance's Way ~ Book Three

Laurel's Choice ~ A Laurel Rowan Story

Romance
Storm's Refuge A Longview Romance Book
One
Come Hell or High Water A Longview
Romance Book Two
A Longview Wedding A Longview Romance
Book Three
A Longview Christmas Seasonal Novella
Kayla's Cowboy A Longview Romance

Arabella's Secret Series
The Selkie's Song ~ Book One

Arabella Dreams ~ Book Two

Co-Authored with Pat Dale
The Last Cowboy
Henrietta's Heart
The Teddy Dialogues
She's Driving Me Crazy

Historical Horror
By N.M. Bell
No Absolution

BWL Publishing

bwlpublishing.ca